touch paper

DAVID FORD

The Book Guild Ltd

First published in Great Britain in 2024 by
The Book Guild Ltd
Unit E2 Airfield Business Park,
Harrison Road, Market Harborough,
Leicestershire. LE16 7UL
Tel: 0116 2792299
www.bookguild.co.uk
Email: info@bookguild.co.uk
X: @bookguild

This work is entirely fictitious and bears no resemblance to any persons living or dead.

Typeset in 10.5pt Adobe Garamond Pro

Printed on FSC accredited paper
Printed and bound in Great Britain by 4edge Limited

ISBN 978 1835740 828

British Library Cataloguing in Publication Data.
A catalogue record for this book is available from the British Library.

Man is not what he thinks he is, he is what he hides.
Andre Malraux

1

The Cabin on the Cliffs

There is a bleak beauty to Homerton Bay. Honey-coloured sand spreads for miles in both directions beneath the imposing cliffs and never-ending sky. It is not the sort of place where crowds come to sunbathe and build sandcastles and only a few hardy locals ever swim in the cold, grey sea. Standing on the cliffs, it is possible to imagine yourself on the barren surface of a distant planet, although the amusement arcades and kiss-me-quick hats of Great Yarmouth are just a short drive away.

The only thing that spoils the view and forces you back to the real world is the burnt-out shell of an old fisherman's cabin that stands on top of the cliffs. Its walls are charred and crumbling, and it is surrounded by weeds.

I noticed the hut a couple of days after I arrived in Homerton. There was something about it that stuck in my mind. Maybe it was the ugliness of the blackened window frames or the stark silhouette of the cabin as the sun went down, but I was intrigued by the building and why it had been left there, like a stain on the landscape.

I had rented a cottage in Homerton-on-Sea (the 'on sea' attracted me) for a few months with the intention of finishing a book I had been promising myself to write. I reckoned the town was far enough away from the distractions of the nearest city to make me focus but that it was a big enough place to have all the essential amenities. It was a quiet, rather melancholy, town with a medieval church, a garage, a handful of shops and a pleasant little tearoom that sold homemade cakes and good coffee.

The quietness I craved soon turned out to be annoying rather than productive and I went off in search of distractions. Every town has it secrets and if there is one thing that distracts a writer it is the prospect of finding those secrets. The locals were friendly enough, but they were wary of outsiders and did not want to talk about the town and its past. They were reluctant to tell me what had caused the fire up on the cliffs and would change the subject when I asked about it.

I went to the cabin a few times when I was out walking. I went to sniff around and to look for clues as to what had happened there but there was nothing much to see. There were burnt patches on the bare ground around it. The metal door was twisted on its hinges. Inside, there was one large room with a couple of smaller ones running off it at one end that had once, presumably, been a kitchen or storage area. The window frames were cremated and two were crudely shuttered with planks of wood. Half the corrugated roof was missing, and the beams were exposed. There were bits of broken shelving and charred furniture and old rags scattered around the place. The concrete floor was strewn with rubbish and there was graffiti on the walls.

I sensed that something terrible had happened in the hut and that it played an important role in the secret that haunted the town. I decided the best place to glean information about the hut and its secrets was the local pub.

The Fisherman's Return is a busy place, popular with both locals and visitors. Late one night, I was standing at the bar when a man stumbled against it. He looked up at me and grinned. He had a long, gaunt face, as if his skull was trying to escape his skin. He was clearly drunk. The barman came round and dragged him to his feet.

'Come on, Tony, you've had enough for tonight.'

He steered him towards the door with his hand on his elbow and pushed him out into the night.

'I'm sick and tired of him,' said the barman, brushing his hands. 'He's a drunken old sod and it would be better for everyone if he pissed off out of here.'

After that, I noticed Tony every time I went into the pub. He was always there. His name was Tony Fletcher and he had lived in the town since he was a boy. He would sit alone, drinking with the determination of an alcoholic, his face lowered as he argued with himself, muttering curses and rubbing the spittle from his lips. If he was fighting his inner demons, it was clearly a bloody, bare-knuckle fight. He was only forty but looked older. Still, he was a striking figure of a man. There was something uncompromising about him, something hard and unyielding. He was tall and powerful, and he had dark, penetrating eyes.

'He didn't always look so grim,' said the young barmaid who noticed me staring at him. 'Apparently, when he was a young man there wasn't a girl in the town who didn't fancy him. Difficult to imagine now, isn't it?' She wiped down the counter. There was a lull in trade, and she was keen to talk, particularly to a fellow outsider. 'People say he's sick in the head. Seems something terrible happened. It was years ago but nobody talks about it, even now. Not to me, anyway. I've been here a year, and they still treat me like a stranger.'

Just then a man entered the pub. He looked as if he carried

all the woes of the world on his shoulders. Tony reached out to him as he passed, grabbing his arm, but the man shook his arm free. He leaned in and said something to Tony. Whatever it was it didn't seem too friendly.

'Who's that?' I asked, nodding towards them.

'That's James Larner. He runs the garage over by the church.'

Tony and the man were having an argument. After a moment, the man left the pub, slamming the door behind him.

'They grew up here together. Part of the same gang and all of that. But as you can see, they're certainly not friends anymore.'

'Do you know if there is anyone else left here, from those days I mean?'

The barmaid shrugged her shoulders. 'I don't know, but I doubt it. Who would want to stay in a craphole like this unless they had to? Anyone with any sense gets out of here as soon as they can.'

'I wonder why they never left,' I mused out loud, thinking about Tony and James Larner.

'Where would a man like that go?' said the barmaid, nodding in Tony's direction. 'His type would always prefer to be a big fish in a small pond.'

The other name that kept coming up was Sullivan. I had first heard it when I picked up the keys to the cottage from the newsagents and the woman who gave them to me muttered something about it being the "Sullivans' old place". Whenever I heard the name after that, it was always muttered or whispered under the breath, like a curse. Clearly, Mr Sullivan had been something of a character, a modern cowboy, and he was talked about in fond way. The other name was that of a woman, Becky Sullivan, and when she was mentioned it was with no hint of fondness.

I had got friendly with the woman who served in the local shop and would talk to her when I picked up my milk and bread in the morning. She was a small, stout woman who was always bustling around. She was a great talker and knew everyone.

'He must have been quite a character,' I ventured one morning. 'The chap who used to own the cottage I'm renting. Pete Sullivan, wasn't it?'

'That's right.'

'Seems he was quite the local celebrity. I guess he didn't leave the town that long ago.'

'Oh, he didn't leave,' said the woman. 'Not in that way, anyhow. The only way Pete Sullivan would ever leave this place was in a coffin. He loved it here. He must have died about fourteen years ago now. Tragic it was, how he went in the end.' I must have looked surprised because she quickly said, 'Everyone round here knew Pete. He was a legend. He was a right rogue, and he liked a few drinks, but he would help anyone out. Generous too. That's why him and his daughter were always skint. He saved the skin of quite a few in this town I can tell you.'

'His daughter? Was that Becky?'

'That's right, Becky Sullivan. She broke her father's heart, she did.'

'Oh, how was that then?'

The woman eyed me suspiciously. 'Let's just say there was always trouble with her and men. Becky was very beautiful, and she knew it. But it was more than that; there was something about her that turned men soft in the head. They would do stupid things around her, and she would encourage them. Even Pete fell for it, and it almost destroyed him in the end. The last time we saw her was after he died. She didn't even bother to come back for his funeral. Mind you, she couldn't wait to sell the cottage quick enough. Even then she caused trouble. I guess she paid for it in the end though.'

Other customers had come into the shop and the woman was relieved to change the subject. She bustled away to serve them saying, 'Well, I can't stand here all day gassing.' But then she turned and said, 'I wouldn't worry too much about that girl and what happened to her. She's something on the TV now apparently. Her sort always land on their feet. It's the people they destroy on the way I feel sorry for. Nobody in this town likes to be reminded of Becky Sullivan, I can tell you.'

If the woman in the shop was chatty, the others in the town were cagey and I might have lost interest in the story if it had not of been for what happened a week later. I was in the pub again when I heard one of the customers, who had had too much to drink, talking loudly to a couple of other men. 'I'll never forgive that bastard for what he did to my Sam. She would still be living here if it wasn't for him. He's a twisted pervert, that's what he is.' He glared over at Tony.

His companions looked embarrassed. They glanced over to see if I had heard. 'Come on, Sandy, that was years ago. He's served his time. Let sleeping dogs lie,' said one of the men, trying to shut him up.

'It don't matter to me. That man is a curse on this town. What he did was evil. They should have left him to rot in prison.'

'Let's not go over that again. The past is past.'

'Not to me it ain't. I wish to God he had died in that bloody fire, I really do.'

What events had disturbed the town so much that they continued to haunt it like this so many years later? What was the connection between Tony Fletcher and Becky Sullivan, if indeed there was any connection at all? I knew then that I would have to tell the story of what had happened in Homerton all those years ago.

2

'You do want money, don't you, Becks?' Tony Fletcher gripped Becky Sullivan's bony shoulder beneath her school blazer. She was thin and the blazer hung off her. Still she looked good in anything, including the stiff school uniform which was designed to remove any individuality from the wearer and make them as dull and unattractive as possible. She still had to wear it even though she was nearly eighteen and doing her A levels in the sixth form.

Tony was nearly three years older than her and even thinner, but in a strong, wiry way. Although he had a job and a car, he did not mind going out with a girl still at school, particularly if she was as good-looking as Becky. Many men much older than him would have jumped at the chance of having a relationship with her. She was a catch.

'You need the money as much as I do,' he said firmly, knowing it was true. 'Your dad pisses away everything up the pub.'

Becky Sullivan lived with her dad in a cottage in Homerton. Her mum had walked out on them a year before and was now living in Norwich. Everyone in Homerton knew Peter Sullivan. He was the local wheeler-dealer and most of his dealing was done in the pub. When he had money he was generous, which meant he never had money for long. The idea of saving anything for the future was alien to him.

'You know I want the money, Tony, but there must be another way to get it.'

Tony pulled her in closer and kissed the top of her head. 'Do you think I would ask you to do that, Becks, if there was alternative? There is no other way. It makes me feel sick to think of you coming on to a man like Palmer, it really does. But you don't have to do anything serious with him. Just enough to hook the bastard and get some evidence. Once he's got a feel of you, he will do anything, I promise you. Any man would. And a young guy like him, well he won't want to jeopardise his career. He'll pay up like a baby just to keep it quiet.'

Tony felt Becky's soft body in his embrace, and it excited him. He lifted her hair and started to kiss her neck. She lowered her head on to her right shoulder and Tony began to nuzzle and bite her ear. She gave a bored sigh and pulled away.

'Oh, Tony, the thought of him kissing me, letting him touch me up. It's so horrible.'

'It won't mean anything, Becks. I know that. You'll be doing it for us.'

'I love you, Tony.' She let his left hand slip inside her blouse.

'Just give him a good time, Becks. Close your eyes and think of the money. When he is ready we will put the screws on him. It will be easy, I promise you.'

Becky and Tony had been going out for nearly a year. He worked at a big bakery in Acle and was often waiting for her in his car when she came out of school. He had gone to the same school himself but had left when he was sixteen. He had been bright but lazy, cheeky and disruptive, and the teachers had been glad to see him go.

Even at school he had done a bit of dealing in drugs and now he was well known as a supplier for miles around.

'I don't like troublemakers like him hanging around the school gates,' said the head of Hemsby High School and College. 'Before you know it, we will have a proper drugs market out there.'

The head got the local police to have a word with Tony and to move him on, but Tony simply started parking in one of the side streets round the corner from the main entrance.

Alistair Palmer had been teaching history at the school for the past two years. He was twenty-five. He and his wife, Sandra, had moved from Birmingham where he had spent two years teaching in a good grammar school. His move to Hemsby High was a promotion and they bought one of the new houses on the outskirts of Homerton. Almost as soon as they arrived in the area, Sandra got pregnant and nine months later she gave birth to twins. The couple had barely had a proper night's sleep since then and this, together with the increased workload that came with his new job, left Alistair Palmer exhausted. This suited his wife, as the trauma of having two babies had completely turned her off sex.

Working in the sixth form could be sexually frustrating for a young teacher like Alistair. Some of the girls openly flaunted their sexuality and they would playfully flirt with him. Alistair had little social life outside of school so, apart from his wife and a couple of her friends, the only women he came across were his fellow teachers and the girls he taught. He fantasised about some of the girls. He could not stop himself. The way they paraded around the school, it was almost as if they invited it.

Late one spring afternoon, Mr Palmer went to pick up some books from his car which he had parked off campus after going out for a rare lunch in a local pub. The sun was shining, and he was still feeling mellow from the two pints of beer he had allowed himself over lunch. He was walking back to his classroom when he noticed Tony Fletcher's car parked in a deserted side road, and he detoured past it. He realised as he drew alongside, that there were people in the car. He could not stop himself from bending down and looking inside as he went past and that's when he saw Tony and Becky in the back seat. Becky was lying across the seat with her skirt pulled up. Tony was bent over beside her, his head half hidden by the skirt as he burrowed between her legs. Becky's eyes were closed. The couple were so transported they did not seem to care that they could be seen. Alistair felt like a peeping tom. He went red with shame and quickly moved on.

Alistair Palmer returned to the classroom in a state of anxiety. The lust of the young couple excited him. He was breathless. He could not get the image of Becky's ecstatic face out of his mind.

*

'You are late, Sullivan,' barked Alistair Palmer as Becky walked into the classroom the next morning. He tapped his watch. It was the day after he had caught her and Tony in the car and he had thought about her all night.

'It's only ten past, sir.'

'That doesn't matter. You are always late, and I am sick of it. I am giving you an hour's detention so you can make up the time you have lost.'

'That's not fair,' said Becky petulantly.

'No. What's not fair is that you cannot be bothered to get to class on time. That's not fair on me, it is not fair on the other students and most of all, Becky, it's not fair on yourself.'

Becky sat down with a huff. Palmer glared at her, as if to say "I'm not finished yet". She did not know why he was being like this. Normally he was a soft touch. She could turn up late and he did not seem to mind. All she had to do was smile at him and he would go all gooey towards her. She knew exactly how to play teachers like him.

But today he was different. For the next hour, Becky could do nothing right. He angrily told her off when he caught her talking to some of the other girls. He tore apart an answer she gave to the class and mocked her in front of her friends.

'If you spent as much time revising as you do tarting yourself up, you might actually achieve something,' said Palmer viciously as he handed her back an unfairly marked essay. It was only when she looked downbeat that he quickly added, 'I am only thinking about you, Becky. I don't want you to waste your life.'

Still Becky hated him. She wanted to humiliate him as he had humiliated her.

That evening she told the gang what had happened. The gang that hung around Homerton consisted of Tony and Becky, her best friend Esther, Stuart Bushell and James Larner. They were pretty much the only people of their age in the town so had been forced together. They would hang around the chip shop and in the cabin up on the cliffs. Only Tony and James were old enough to go to the pub.

Nobody but Tony could be the leader of the group. He was earning good money, and he could do what he liked. He lived alone with his mother, who was slowly drinking herself to death. She had been an emotional wreck ever since his dad had left them ten years ago. Tony despised his mother. He thought she was weak and pathetic. He hated the way she talked to her three cats like they were babies. Tony often thought that if she had shown his dad as much affection as she showed her cats, he might have stayed.

The group did whatever Tony said. Only James had the confidence to stand up to Tony but usually all he wanted was a quiet life and whenever there was any argument or conflict he would just walk away.

James was nineteen. Like Tony, he had left school at sixteen. His mum had died when he was just thirteen and he needed to help his dad run the garage and to look after his brother Nick, who was what people politely called "slow". Nick was a year younger than James but had the mental age of an eight-year-old. James's dad was never around much anymore. He found having Nick for a son and trying to run the garage a strain and so was increasingly away, saying he had business to do in Norwich, though James could never work out what the business was or why it required him to stay overnight.

Stuart Bushell was the puppy in the group, the runt of the pack if you wanted to be unkind. He was always sucking up to Tony and was both a little bit infatuated and scared of him. Secretly, he lusted after Becky.

The group's notoriety with the old people of Homerton was far greater than anything they actually did. Most nights they just hung around the village green or the mini-market or went drinking up on the dunes. On that evening, they were piled into the bus stop across from the church.

'You saw it, didn't you, Est?' said Becky. 'He was so mean. It's like he deliberately wanted to make me feel small.'

'He's always like that with some of us,' said Esther. She was dark and petite and pretty but was shy and awkward with boys and had never had a boyfriend. Being Becky's best friend meant she was always in her shadow and Esther quite liked that. She was easily the brightest one in the group, and she came across as quiet and studious. She was studying hard for her A levels and was desperate to get away to university. She had known Becky since they were infants together and they trusted and respected each other, despite being such different characters.

'He always was a bastard,' said Tony, though Palmer had never taught him.

'He wasn't,' said James. 'He was one of the best teachers in the school. He was really kind about my brother.'

'Not everything revolves round your bloody brother,' said Tony. 'People are only kind to him because they feel sorry for him. The fact is Palmer was horrible to Becky and we should teach him a lesson and get our own back.' Tony looked across at Becky for her approval, but she was muttering something to Esther. 'We could go round and piss him off a bit,' said Tony. 'Why should he have a nice cosy night in when we are stuck out here. Let's go and mess him up.'

'What are you talking about?' said Esther, bemused.

Stuart giggled. 'We could tip out his bins. Throw dog shit into his garden. Keep ringing his doorbell.'

'Jesus! Are you two five?' said Esther. 'The poor bloke has got young babies for Christ's sake. Give him a break.'

'I agree,' said James.

'There's a surprise,' said Stuart. 'If it was up to you, we would never do anything.'

'And you think ringing someone's doorbell is doing something? Why don't you grow up, Stuart.'

After a few minutes, James and Tony got some cans of lager from the minimart and they all went down to the beach to watch the sunset. They made a fire out of driftwood and sat huddled around it.

'You seemed pretty angry with Palmer earlier,' whispered Tony to Becky. He had his arm round her. Her face was lit up by the fire. 'Does that mean you are going ahead with our plan?'

'I'm still not sure. It seems quite a big thing to do.'

Tony looked over at the others. Esther was lying between Stuart and James. They were talking about some comedy programme on the TV.

'We've got to do something, Becks. We're not like them,' said Tony. 'We want more than this don't we?' Tony squeezed Becky against his side. 'We don't want to leave it too late. If we are going to do it, we need to do it now.'

*

Alistair Palmer was a popular member of the teaching staff, and he got on well with his colleagues. The male teachers in the school were a close-knit group and they had made Alistair feel welcome from the start, though some of them envied his youth and a couple resented the fact he had got the head-of-department role instead of themselves. He seemed to have everything: youth, good looks, a wife and young family, a good career ahead of him. Still, he could take a joke and stood his round on Friday night when they went for a few drinks after work.

'Look at poor old Palmer there. He's so dog-tired, he could sleep anywhere. Even if there was a naked woman next to him he'd be asleep.' Mr Crosby of class five laughed as he rubbed his glasses clean. Alistair Palmer, who had dozed off for a minute, woke with a start in a chair in the staffroom.

'Is that right Alistair,' roared Mr Dennison, 'you would literally sleep with any woman?'

'What on earth do you mean?' spluttered Palmer.

'You being so knackered, lad,' said Mr Dennison. 'We know it can't be easy with two young babies keeping you up half the night. Nobody blames you for wanting a bit of shut-eye.'

'I wouldn't mind sleeping with her,' muttered Mr Crosby, peering out of the staffroom window down on to the school entrance. All of the male teachers knew Becky Sullivan and most of them found her attractive. Quite a few had fantasised about her in the privacy of their own beds. Beautiful young girls like her were a constant reminder to the male teachers in the school that they were not young anymore.

'What?' said Dennison, joining him at the window.

'Oh nothing, just dreaming,' said Crosby. He nodded down at the school gates. 'That girl will break a few hearts when she's older, I can tell you.' Dennison gave him a knowing smile.

'You know she's going out with that troublemaker Tony Fletcher?' said Crosby.

'I'd heard. Her old man's a bit dodgy as well. Between them the poor girl doesn't stand a chance.'

It was when the bailiffs turned up at the cottage one morning as she was leaving for school that Becky decided to go ahead with the plan to seduce and blackmail Mr Palmer. They thumped on the door and squeezed their fat faces through the letterbox demanding to be let in. 'We've got a warrant,' they threatened. 'You can let us in like a good girl or we can kick the door down.' Her father was nowhere to be seen and Becky was scared. She let the men in and watched them walk out with the TV, DVD player and stereo.

That afternoon, Becky met Tony after school. He was standing by a wall near his car. He was throwing stones at something in one of the back gardens. Becky crept up behind him and kissed him on the neck. He turned round, startled.

'What ya doing?' asked Becky.

Tony nodded in the direction of the garden and launched another stone. 'Just trying to get that fat, ugly moggie to move.'

'I've got some news, Tony.'

'Let's hear it then.'

'I've decided we should do it. You know the Palmer thing. I think we should go ahead.'

'Are you sure, Becks?'

'Yeh, why not. I need some money and I can't think how else we are going to get it, can you?'

'We will need to do it properly,' said Tony. He was distracted, thinking things through in his head. After a moment he turned to Becky with a serious look on his face. He gripped her hand hard. 'We'll need to start it off slow, kinda hook him in. We need to drag it out a bit, so we got proof. The more evidence we can get the better; notes from him, pictures, messages, that sort of thing. Anything that incriminates him. The more we've got the more he will pay up.'

'He's not stupid, Tony. He will be careful. You know what he's like.'

'He will be so into you that he won't know what he is doing.'

'But he won't want to risk his job. He might not think it's worth it. He could report me.'

'He won't do that, Becky. Believe me. I know his sort. He's pervy. He'll do anything to get inside your knickers. We just need to play it right. Be discreet at first so he feels safe. Make him think you really fancy him, that you think he is special.'

'What if he doesn't fancy me?'

Tony laughed. 'Don't be silly, Becks. I know men. He will definitely want to fuck you.'

3

'Are you coming for the bus?' asked Esther, packing her books into her backpack.

'Not tonight,' said Becky.

'Is Tony picking you up?'

'No. I thought I'd do some work in the library. Try and catch up a bit. Palmer was right in a way. I don't want to mess up these A levels. It's the only chance we've got to get away from here.'

'Do you want me to stay with you?'

'No, it's OK. You'll just distract me.'

Esther and Becky were walking along the corridor. They stopped in front of the library. Becky seemed reluctant to go in.

'Are you sure you are OK, Becks? You seem a little on edge.'

'Oh, Est, I hope I'm not doing the wrong thing. I feel as if I'm making a big mistake.'

'What do you mean?' Esther took Becky's hand. 'Tony's not making you do stuff is he? Stuff you don't want to do?'

'It's not that,' said Becky. She shook herself down. 'I am just being silly. I guess I'm just worried about the exams. You get off, I'll see you later,' she said brightly. Becky went to enter the library but turned and said, 'You will stick by me, won't you, Est? Whatever happens, we will always be friends, won't we? As long as I know that, I can cope with anything.'

Becky leant back against the cold corridor wall and took a deep breath. In a few minutes there would be no turning back. She kept telling herself it was no big deal but suddenly it felt as if it was. She told herself that she was doing it for her and Tony and that there was no other way. She could hear his voice, jabbing away inside her head, saying what a dirty little pervert he was for eyeing up all the schoolgirls and how he deserved to be taught a lesson, and how everything would be OK. Becky was confused now as to why she was doing this. Was it to punish him or for the money? She convinced herself they could both benefit. Palmer would get some sex and she would make some money. It was no different from what happened every Saturday night in the clubs of Great Yarmouth. If he wanted her, he would have to pay for it. It no longer sounded like extortion. No one would get hurt, not really. It was a just a game. She counted to three then stepped inside the classroom.

Alistair Palmer was marking books. It was half-past-four and the school was silent except for the whirr of Mr Paxton's polisher as it swept from side to side along the corridor floors.

Becky entered and stood by the door, looking at Mr Palmer. His head was bowed down over his desk, and he was sucking the end of his pen.

His head jerked up. 'Ah, Becky. I thought you'd left ages ago.'

'I was doing homework in the library,' she said, moving tentatively forward between the tables. 'I think I left my history book in here.'

They both glanced over at the thick book on the shelf by the window. 'Looks as if you were right,' said Mr Palmer.

Becky stroked her hair and smiled at him. He noticed the top two buttons of her white blouse were undone and he could see the lacey edge of her bra beneath. Becky went over to the shelf. Mr Palmer returned to the books on his desk to try and distract himself but now she was in his head, and he could not shake off the thought of her soft, white breasts. He caught a hint of Becky's perfume from across the room.

Without knowing why, Mr Palmer pushed back his chair and stood up. He felt a bit shaky. He moved round to the front of the desk as if he was going to fetch something from one of the tables. As he did so, he glanced over at Becky, who was leaning back against the windowsill.

'Hadn't you better be getting home?' Mr Palmer asked. His voice was a little hoarse.

'No rush. My dad won't be home for ages. I get lonely in the cottage by myself.' She arched her back a little so that her chest pressed against her blouse. It was pointing straight at Mr Palmer. 'I'm not disturbing you am I, sir?'

'No, of course not. It's quiet in here. Too quiet sometimes.' He did not know why he was babbling like this.

'I could sit here and read my book,' said Becky.

She had moved without him noticing and was now brushing past him, gently cornering him against the table. He felt her hand skim his arm. He could smell her perfume strongly now.

'You look hot, sir.' She smoothed down the front of her skirt knowing his eyes would follow the movement of her hand. Was she doing this deliberately? Was she flirting with him? *The little tart*, thought Mr Palmer. *God, I could teach her a lesson!*

'It must be kind of boring,' said Becky. 'Marking books all the time.' She stretched languorously, raising her arms above her head. 'You should have some fun.'

He thought carefully before he answered and tried to sound matter of fact. 'I don't do too bad.'

'With two babies at home I guess you prefer being here, huh?'

Mr Palmer baulked at the mention of his children. For some reason he had not expected her to know about them but then he reckoned, why not? They were not a secret, and everybody knew everything about everybody around here.

'I guess I do,' he said light-heartedly. She was teasing him and it made him angry, but he also liked it.

Becky looked at him straight on and he did not turn away. He was breathing hard. Her face was a few inches in front of his. Her breasts were heaving beneath her blouse. 'I like you, sir,' she said, nibbling her bottom lip. 'I really like you.' She reached out and took his hand and placed it on her blouse. She knew she had him.

'We shouldn't.' Mr Palmer gasped. 'You know it's not right.' But he did not pull his hand away.

Becky did not say anything. On tiptoe, she leaned forward and kissed him. 'It's too late to stop now,' she whispered.

Afterwards, Becky ran to the girl's loos and threw up. Then she felt better, as if she had purged the memory of what had just happened down the toilet bowl. *The important thing*, she told herself, *is not to think about what I am doing.*

Alistair Palmer went to the staffroom. He scrubbed his neck with soap and hot water where Becky had kissed him, worried that the smell of her mouth would cling to his skin like a bite.

'You are working late,' said a voice as Palmer came out into the staffroom. It was Dennison. He was sitting in a corner of the room, marking books. He looked over the top of his glasses. 'Don't let the bastards grind you down, Alistair.'

Had Dennison been there when he dashed into the staffroom after the incident with Becky? He could not be sure. Alistair felt a flush of guilt redden his face. 'Guess so,' he stuttered.

20

'Suppose you are not too keen to get back to those screaming babies of yours?' joked Dennison. 'I've just seen that Becky Sullivan going home,' he said, nodding towards the window. The nosey bugger was always spying on people through the staffroom window. 'It's not like her to hang around school any longer than she has too. Still, the world's loss is our gain.'

Alistair sensed that Dennison was probing him. That he knew something but wanted to confirm the truth by tripping him up. He was teasing out a confession. Alistair started to think of alibis.

'Oh really? I haven't seen a soul. There was nobody around my block. She's probably just waiting for that boyfriend of hers.'

'A girl like her could do better than that Fletcher. She could have men falling over her.'

Alistair pretended not to understand. 'Really? She never struck me as that attractive. I can't see the appeal myself.' Alistair cleared his throat. 'Gosh is that the time? I'd better get home to the wife.' And he dashed out like a boy with stolen sweets in his pockets.

4

Over the next couple of weeks, Becky and Tony put their plan into action. Tony liked to think he was in control and would tell Becky exactly what she had to do. Most of the time she did not listen. She was uncomfortable discussing it with Tony and besides, she knew what was required. Becky would leave a note on Mr Palmer's desk when she could stay behind after school and each time she allowed him to go a bit further, but never too far.

Mr Palmer would pretend to be busy but as soon as Becky entered the classroom he would jump up from his chair and say, 'You came,' in such a grateful voice that Becky knew he had been sitting looking at the door ever since the last class had finished. In fact, the thought of her arrival would often create such a state of desire all through his afternoon classes, that he was unable teach properly and would tell his students to sit and read through their textbooks. It was the same each time, as if he could never quite believe it when she turned up as promised. Of course, he kept telling himself not to be there, to leave at half-past-three and go home, but he could not stop himself. His desire for Becky was so great, he had no choice but to see her again. There was never much conversation between them. Alistair would lock the classroom door and pull down the blinds. Becky would lean against one of the tables and he would go over and kiss her. She rationed what he could do to her, and she made sure to finish before he got too excited. 'You just want what you can't have,' she told Palmer.

Alistair was besotted with her. He could not sleep at nights from thinking about her. In school he was distracted. Some of the other teachers noticed and asked what was wrong but he would just say it was nothing or that the babies had not slept the night before.

Becky had three classes with Mr Palmer every week. Becky turned up late to the first lesson after she had kissed him, and Alistair Palmer fumbled a mild admonishment. He could not look her in the face. 'I'm really sorry, sir,' she said, 'but I couldn't sleep last night. It was so hot.' She brushed her hand under the collar of her blouse, opened her mouth slightly and ran her tongue around her lips. After that, she flirted with him in each lesson, winking at him when no one was looking, touching her hair and the bottom of her neck, asking suggestive questions about the historic figures they were studying. A couple of times, Alistair gave her little notes attached to her essays that said things like, *I can't stop thinking about you* and *I love naughty girls*.

Late at night, Becky would send Alistair flirtatious texts and encouraged him to do the same to her. *I'm all alone in bed with nothing on. What would you like to do to me right now?*

'Who keeps messaging you at this time of night?' said Sandra sleepily. She rolled over. 'It's bad enough with the babies keeping us up half the night.' Her voice trailed off as she dozed back to sleep.

'It's nothing. Just work,' Alistair mumbled. *I'd kiss you all over*, he texted.

Ping went his phone. *Would you like to fuck me?*

Oh yes. As soon as he sent it, he regretted it. How could he be so stupid.

His phone pinged again. It was a picture of Becky blowing him a kiss. The message said: *Tell me what time we can meet tomorrow.* Alistair was so scared he closed his phone and put it on the bedside cabinet. He turned off the side light and lay in the darkness. He was too worried to sleep. He kept looking at the phone and thinking how he could undo what he had just done.

*

The next time they met after school, Becky was sullen and when Alistair tried to kiss her, she pulled away. He grabbed her wrist. 'What is it?' he asked.

'I thought you liked me, sir.'

'I do, Becky. Of course I do.'

'Then why are you blanking me. You don't you return my messages anymore. I like it when you talk dirty to me. And I thought you liked me sending you sexy little messages.'

'You know I do, but it's just too risky that's all. My wife, she looks at my phone sometimes. If we are not careful, someone will find our texts. God knows who you share your phone with.'

'I like a bit of risk. It's sexy,' said Becky. She nodded towards the door. 'We could leave it unlocked sometimes.'

'We've got to be sensible, Becky. This isn't a game. If anyone found out, I could go to prison. They'd do me for abuse of trust. I would never work again. It's different for you. You wouldn't tell anyone, would you, Becky, not even that friend of yours, Esther? I know you are close.'

Becky turned away.

'You've got to promise me, Becky. You've got to keep this a secret. If anyone found out I don't know what I would do.'

'That depends, sir. I'd be so upset if we broke up. People are bound to ask what was wrong.'

'That sounds like a threat,' said Alistair tersely.

Becky realised she had overstepped the mark. She forced out a nervous laugh. 'Course not. I wouldn't do anything to hurt you. I thought you knew that. I really like you. I want us to be like a proper couple. I wouldn't be doing this otherwise.'

'I'm not sure we should be doing *this* anymore. It's not right, Becky. We should stop it now before we go too far. We should just forget what has happened. I think we should stop seeing each other, alone that is.'

Becky ran her fingernail along the back of Alistair's hand. She pecked him on the cheek. 'You don't mean that. You don't really want to forget about those lovely things we did. The way we touch each other. You're crazy about me, aren't you, sir?'

Palmer looked anxious.

'What's the matter?' asked Becky. 'Aren't I sexy enough for you? We can do more if you like, I promise.'

Alistair was overwhelmed with desire. 'What sort of things?' he asked hoarsely.

'Well wouldn't you like to find out,' teased Becky. 'But you've got to promise me we won't break up. I'm not some slag who sleeps with anyone, you know.'

*

The next day, as Becky was leaving his class, Mr Palmer called after her, asking if she could stay behind for a few minutes.

'I'll be with you in a sec,' Becky said to Esther.

'I've got something for you,' said Alistair and he handed her a small, neatly wrapped package. 'I've been thinking about what I said to you yesterday and I am sorry. Of course, I want us to carry on.'

Becky unwrapped the present. It was a beautiful silver bracelet. She slipped it on her wrist, admiring it. Then she pulled out her phone. She leaned over and kissed Alistair on the cheek. 'Thank you, Alistair,' she said as she kissed him again with her braceleted hand caressing his cheek. She took a picture.

'I wish you hadn't done that,' said Alistair. 'Please delete it, Becky. Please, I am begging you.'

Alistair's wife and the other teachers noticed a change in his behaviour. He was unsettled and nervous. He was full of guilt and self-loathing. He was constantly worried that someone would find out about his relationship with Becky. But that did not stop him carrying it on.

'I told you never to call me at home,' hissed Alistair, cupping his hands round his phone. Becky could hear the babies crying in the background. 'This is not a good time,' said Alistair. He looked towards the door of the nursery to make sure Sandra was not coming.

'But I've missed you so much. I can't stop thinking about you. I wanted to hear your voice.'

*

Sandra shouted up from downstairs, 'Who the hell are you talking to, Alistair? Can't you sort the bleeding kids out? What the fuck are you doing?' She sounded frazzled.

There was noise coming at him from all directions: his wife screaming at him from the kitchen, the babies wailing on the other side of the nursery and Becky talking seductively on the phone.

Alistair went over to placate the twins, cradling the phone between his neck and shoulder. 'I've got to go, Becky,' he said.

'Tell me you love me first,' demanded Becky.

'I love you.'

'And that you'll do anything I ask.'

26

'Yes, yes. I adore you.'

When Becky told Tony about the phone call, she was surprised by his reaction. 'What did you do that for, Becky? I didn't ask you to call him did I? You shouldn't have called when he was with his kiddies, for Christ's sake.'

'It was only a bit of fun,' said Becky. 'I think he's ready now.'

'Good,' said Tony. 'Because I think you're starting to enjoy this too much. You were just meant to lead him on a bit, Becks, not be a fucking slut. If I didn't know you, I'd think you actually wanted to fuck the guy.'

'Course I don't, Tony. I only want you.'

'Good. Then it's time we put old Palmer out of his misery.'

The next day, Tony got the gang together at the fisherman's cabin to tell them about the plan. He had decided the game was over and now was the time to get serious.

'It will be a piece of piss,' he said. 'We will get old Palmer up here and we will demand he pays the money or else.'

'Or else what?' asked James.

'Or else we will tell the authorities all about him and Becky and what a dirty little boy he's been. We've got the evidence: photos, messages, the lot. You don't buy your pupils presents for Christ's sake, not unless you feel guilty about something.'

James looked over at Becky. 'And what about her? How's she going to feel if everyone knows she has been sleeping with her teacher?'

'I haven't slept with him,' protested Becky. 'I've only led him on a bit.'

'How could you?' said Esther.

'It won't come to that,' Tony snapped. 'That bastard's got too much to lose to risk it all coming out. Now it's payback time.'

When Tony opened the door at home, it smelt of cats' piss. His mum was lying on the sofa in front of the TV, with the cats curled up on her stomach. There was a half-empty bottle of gin on the floor next to the sofa.

'You could at least drink out of a cup,' said Tony. 'It makes you look like a tramp, drinking out of the bottle like that.' The room was a mess, and he made a feeble attempt at tidying it up. He picked the bottle up and put it on a table, out of arm's reach.

'It would just mean extra dishes.'

'Why would you care about that?' said Tony. 'You never do them. This place is disgusting. There's cat food and cat crap everywhere.' He swiped one of the cats off his mother, knocking it to the floor. 'I'm sick of it. We live in a pigsty and you're the fat pig. No wonder Dad left you.'

His mother laughed. 'He left you too, darling. Remember that.' This made Tony angry.

'I hate you,' he shouted. 'You're not a proper mother. Look at you. I'll get my own back one day. I promise you.' He kicked the cat out of the way. 'I'm going to the pub,' he said. 'Hopefully you will be comatose by the time I get back.'

*

One Tuesday evening when Alistair got home from work, he found Sandra throwing some clothes into a bag in bedroom. At first, he thought she might be kicking him out of the house but then saw they were her clothes. He kissed her on top of her head. 'Are you going somewhere?'

'It's Judy,' said Sandra without turning round. 'She phoned earlier. She's having some problems with her Tom, and I said I'd go and keep her company for a few days.' Judy was an old friend from her university days who lived in Norwich. 'I'm sure you won't mind will you?' she said frostily. 'You seem so distracted of late; I might as well not be here anyway.'

Alistair tried to hide his joy. This was an opportunity to spend some real time with Becky. 'If you've got to go, love, you've got to go.' He tried to sound disappointed but there was a smirk on his face. 'I've got stacks of work to do anyway. This will be a chance for me to catch up on my marking.'

Palmer could hardly contain his excitement when the other students left, and he was at last alone again with Becky.

'My wife has gone away for a couple of nights,' he blurted out. His hand was trembling when he touched Becky's arm. 'She's gone to see a friend in Norwich. She's taken the kids.' He whooped with joy.

Parents love their children, thought Becky, *but they love getting shot of them even more.*

'We could spend some proper time together,' said Alistair.

Becky sensed the pleading in his voice and snorted. 'When the wife's away…'

'I want us to be alone,' Alistair said. He sweated desperation.

'I could come back to your house,' Becky teased. She licked his ear with her tongue. 'We could make love in your bed.' She watched his face turn red. 'Or better still, in the little babies' room.'

'Not there. We couldn't do it there. There must be somewhere else.'

Becky pulled away and stood in front of him. 'Not tonight, you naughty boy. I'm busy tonight. But tomorrow. I promise.' She gave him a wet, lingering kiss. 'Come up to the old fisherman's cabin on the cliffs. You know the one. There will be nobody there. Just us two. I'll make sure you have a good time.' She let his hand brush against her breast. 'We've waited so long. Just think how good it will be. Come up there at eight. I will be waiting for you.'

Tony was in the car. 'It's all sorted,' said Becky, kissing him hard on the lips.

5

Alistair Palmer now regretted having the scotch and soda in the Fisherman's Return. Instead of calming him down as intended, it increased his anxiety. He had hardly eaten a thing all day. All he could think about was what might happen that night in the cabin up on the cliffs. He kept asking himself whether this was a cruel prank Becky was playing on him, that he would turn up at the hut and find no one there. It was madness, meeting in a derelict shack in the darkness of night like a pair of desperate teenagers. It was just so sordid. But what if it was really going to happen; what if he was finally going to make love to Becky? For it felt like love to Alistair. He could not stop thinking about Becky. He adored her. The thought of her body sent him wild with desire. He knew he had no choice but to go to the hut that night, no matter how degrading it might turn out to be. He could not resist the chance of sleeping with Becky and he would accept any risk to do so. The thought of having sex with her made him blind to any consequences.

But he was scared. The alcohol pounded through his veins and his heart was racing. His empty stomach was a knot of fear and excitement. He stopped and steadied himself against the wall of a cottage.

The sun was slowly setting, and the town was bathed in soft, orange light. The white stone cottages glowed, as if warmed by a distant fire. A group of five girls came along the road. They had clearly come from the beach. Their long, skinny legs were bare, and they wore flip-flops on their feet. They wore tee shirts and towels and rugby shirts thrown over their shoulders like the arms of a young man. They were laughing and talking loudly, drunk on a day in the sun. Alistair watched their fresh faces as they passed and each one became the face of Becky, a face that was light-hearted and unburdened. He wanted her more than ever. He wanted to feel her youthfulness in his arms.

It was a beautiful summer's evening. The creaking clock on the old Methodist chapel showed it was half-past-seven. A voice said, 'Are you alright, Mr Palmer?' It was Mrs Haylett. Alistair taught her daughter, Samantha, in the lower school.

Alistair jerked his head in Mrs Haylett's direction. 'Yes, thank you.'

She was standing with two carrier bags of shopping at her feet. 'It's a gorgeous evening isn't it?' Alistair nodded. 'You don't want to be cooped up on an evening like this, do you?'

Alistair straightened up and started to leave. 'Where are you off to then?'

'Oh, I thought I would go for a walk up on the dunes. Catch the sunset,' said Alistair.

'Sounds lovely. You don't want to stay up there too long, mind. It gives me the creeps it does, up there after dark. You never know who you might come across do you? And you know what they say?'

'What?' said Alistair, a mite impatiently.

'No one would hear you scream.' Mrs Haylett gave a little chuckle. She picked up her bags. 'Still, must be off. Mr Haylett will be wanting his supper. Enjoy your walk.'

Alistair watched Mrs Haylett hobble along the road. He wished he had not told her he was going up on to the cliffs. He did not want anybody to know what he was doing that night.

The setting sun filled the hut with warm, golden light and the five figures within it were caught, like figures in a Flemish altarpiece. Tony, James and Stuart were pacing around the cabin like athletes before a race. Becky and Esther were sitting together on a battered old sofa. There was a mix of chairs and crates scattered around the main room and the rotten remains of a carpet. One wall was lined with metal shelves. In the small adjoining rooms, there was still a sink and cupboards with their doors hanging off. It must have been fifteen years since the cabin had last been used for work and it had been left to slowly turn to ruin. It had been taken over by successive generations of the town's teenagers, who used it as a place to go and drink, to make out and to escape the prying eyes of the local nosey parkers. Some of the youngsters had even bought things up to the hut to make it feel more like their own space. There were curling posters on the walls, camp lights for when it got dark, even a portable barbecue that could be filled with driftwood to provide warmth on cold nights.

'You'd better turn those on,' said Tony to Stuart. He pointed at two battery-powered camping lamps on the shelf. 'We don't want him to think there is no one here and turn tail.' Stuart did as he was told. 'So, we are all clear what is going to happen are we?' said Tony, more to himself than the others. 'When Palmer comes in, James and Stuart will grab him and hold him down on the chair over there. We will say we know all about his dirty little secret and Becky will confirm what he has done. We will tell him he has got a choice – either he gives us money to stay quiet or we will go and tell his bosses what a pervert he is. He won't be able to run away with all of us here.'

32

'I don't like it. It's not just blackmail, it's assault,' said James. 'We could get in serious trouble over this.'

'Not as much trouble as him,' said Tony.

'We're not bleeding kidnapping him,' said Stuart.

'Aren't we? Sounds like it to me. Sounds like we are mugging him as well. And what if he says he can't pay, or he says he will pay but doesn't? What are we going to do then?'

'You are making this sound more difficult than it is,' Tony said. 'He's been a naughty boy, and he should pay for it. And he will, he just needs a bit of persuading.'

James snorted. 'You know it's not like that, Tony. This is wrong. He will be petrified about losing his job. I don't want to scare him like that.' He looked over at Esther for support, but she was sitting in a daze. She had blanked out why she was there. It was too bizarre to comprehend.

'You're a fucking coward,' spat Tony, glaring at James. 'If you don't want Palmer to get what he deserves, then you can fuck off out of here.' Tony shoved James hard on the shoulders. He pushed him towards the door. 'Go on, get out of here now.'

James scrambled at the door. 'You're mad,' he said. 'You'll regret this, I'm telling you.'

Tony bundled him out of the cabin. 'If you tell anyone about this, I'll kill you. I swear I will.' Tony slammed the door closed. He was seething with anger. 'You had better check the coast is clear,' he ordered Stuart. He turned to Becky. 'Text Palmer and tell him you are here and waiting,' he said.

There were the remains of a Second World War gun shelter near the top of the path that led up to the cliffs and Alistair Palmer stopped there. He looked at the message from Becky. So, she was there! She was waiting for him. Alistair could hardly believe it was true. Walking across the staithes, he had convinced himself it was all a joke and that he would find the old shack empty, but no, Becky was actually there, waiting to

33

make love to him. He tried to picture her waiting. He imagined what she was wearing, whether she was smoking, whether she was as excited by the prospect of them being together as he was. He had never been inside the hut before, although he had passed it on the way down to the beach. He had no idea what it was like inside, but it did not matter. All that mattered was that he and Becky would be alone together.

It was nearly dark now. Alistair felt uncomfortable being up in the dunes at night. There were signs warning people about adders and there had been rumours and stories in the local paper about sightings of wild cats and feral dogs roaming around the staithes. Alistair could feel his heart pounding. He was in such a state of tension, he felt ready to snap like a rubber band. He breathed in deeply to try to calm himself but this just made him more conscious of the blood pounding through his veins.

James saw Palmer leaning against the bunker. He did not look well. Palmer was only a few years older than he was, but standing there, he looked like a wheezing old man who had stopped to catch his breath.

He's not a bad bloke, thought James. He was a good teacher, better than most of those who had taught him. And who could blame him for being seduced by Becky? He was young and she was a sexy and beautiful young woman. She could get any man to do anything she wanted, and she knew it. James hated that part of her.

James knew he should warn Palmer about what was going to happen. He did not deserve to be threatened by that bastard Tony. If he warned him off, hopefully Palmer would go home and nothing would happen. Then Becky and Tony might realise their plan was not going to work and abandon it. That would teach Tony a lesson! But what if Palmer reported them to the police for blackmail? The police would want to question him about it and James knew he would not be able to cope with that. He did not care about Tony, but he would not want to see Becky get into trouble. He adored her.

Alistair Palmer started up the hill and James watched him go. He could have run after him, but he did not. Instead, he remained cowering behind the bush as it grew dark. James despised his weakness, his cowardice.

'You can leave it to Stuart and me,' said Tony to Becky and Esther. 'In fact, it might be better if you weren't around. If things turn nasty, it would be better if you weren't here.' Tony looked around. He decided it was too late now for the girls to leave the cabin. 'Go and hide in there until it's all over,' he said indicating the side room.

When they had gone, Tony tossed a pair of gloves over to Stuart. 'Here, put these on. If things get a bit rough, we don't want to leave any evidence.'

Three yellow rectangles shone faintly in the darkness. Alistair reached the top of the cliffs and the night sky brightened. He could hear the roaring of the waves below. As he moved closer to the cabin, he could see the lamps glowing inside. It was too late to turn back now.

The metal door of the cabin was slightly open. Alistair hesitated. 'Becky, are you there?' There was no answer. 'Becky, it's me,' said Alistair, louder this time. He pushed open the door.

Stuart grabbed Alistair as soon as he came inside. He spun him around and shoved him into the chair, shouting, 'Gotcha!'

'Where's Becky?' demanded Alistair in the confusion.

'Wouldn't you like to know.' Stuart gave a little dance. 'You pervert,' he shouted. He pinned Alistair down on the chair, his hands pressing against Alistair's shoulders.

'What the fuck are you doing?' said Alistair. He glared at Tony.

'You've been a naughty boy, haven't you?' said Tony. 'A very naughty boy.'

'This is nothing to do with you,' pleaded Alistair. 'It's between Becky and me.'

Tony laughed. 'You think so? You really think so?'

Alistair tried to stand up, but Stuart pushed him back. 'You do what we say now.'

'Just ask her. She told me to come here.'

'And why do you think she did that?' said Tony.

'You better not have hurt her. I'm warning you.'

'Listen,' said Tony, pushing his own face an inch in front of Alistair's. 'You don't get it, do you? We know what you've done, you disgusting pervert. We've got all the evidence, and you are going to pay for it, you really are.'

'I don't know what you are talking about.' Panic washed across his face.

'Of course you do,' sneered Tony. 'Becky made sure she kept those little love notes of yours, those late-night texts you sent her, the photos. You should have been more careful; a clever man like you.'

'I want to speak to her,' said Alistair. 'We can work something out. She wouldn't do this to me.'

'She was in on it from the start,' said Stuart. 'Why else would she go with a bloke like you? You don't seriously think she found you attractive, do you?'

Tony knelt down so his face was level with Alistair's. They were almost chin to chin. 'Now, this is how it is going to work,' he said menacingly. 'You are going to pay us five hundred quid to keep our mouths shut. Then you are going to keep paying us to stay silent.' He stood up and said to Stuart, 'What do you think, Stu? How much do you think a pervert like Palmer here can afford? A hundred quid a week should do it, eh?'

'I can't,' pleaded Palmer.

'You can't what?'

'I haven't got that sort of money. I can't find a hundred quid a week, I just can't. I don't have it. I've got a mortgage and family.'

Stuart laughed. 'Did you hear that, Tone. The poor man has got a mortgage.'

'It's up to you,' said Tony. 'Either you pay up or we tell the authorities what you've been doing. They don't take too kindly to teachers playing around with their students do they? You'll lose your job for sure. You may even go to prison. Who'll pay your mortgage then?'

'Palmer the paedo, that's what they'll call him.' Stuart chuckled.

'This is blackmail,' Palmer stuttered. His face was flushed, and beads of sweat were running down his forehead. His palms were clammy. It felt as if his head was about to explode.

'And who are you going to tell?' said Stuart, hopping around. 'Are you going to tell the cops you are being blackmailed because you are sleeping with a schoolgirl?' He and Tony laughed.

Alistair felt faint. The blood burst in his veins. His vision blurred. 'I need to go.'

'You're not going anywhere,' barked Tony.

'Please. I beg you. I'll pay. I will. But I need time.'

'We want the money tonight. You can get it from the cash machine at the minimart.'

'I don't have it.' He felt as if he was going to black out. 'I'll get it for you tomorrow. I promise.'

'No way. We need some of it tonight or you're not leaving.' Tony took out his phone. 'I think it's about time we called that wife of yours and told her your dirty secret.'

'He looks as if he's going to wet himself,' said Stuart.

Alistair bent forward, as if gripped by a sudden pain. He

clutched at his chest. He toppled off the chair and fell on to the floor with a thud. He was bent double. His face turned a deathly white, his eyes bulged. His body jerked a couple of times, his leg kicking out. His mouth opened in a gasp. He shuddered then lay limply on the floor.

'Fucking hell!' screamed Stuart. He glanced over to Tony for reassurance, but Tony was standing there rigidly looking down at the body. The blood had drained from his face. His mouth was open in horror.

'What have we done?' screeched Stuart. 'What the fuck have we done?'

Becky and Esther came running into the room. 'What's going on?' demanded Becky. Then they saw Palmer's body lying on the floor. Esther screamed.

'Jesus, what did you do to him?' said Becky, turning from Tony to Stuart. She went towards the body.

'Don't touch him,' Tony ordered. He did not move. He did not turn to look Becky in the eye.

'What if he is still alive?'

'It's too late for that,' said Tony. His voice was flat and unemotional. It was as if a machine was speaking.

'We have to call an ambulance. We've got to. We can't just leave him like this. We need to get help.' Becky was babbling. Her hands were shaking uncontrollably. She looked at Stuart, then at Esther. Stuart was rocking his head from side to side in shock. He kept muttering, 'Fucking hell, fucking hell.' One hand was screwed inside the other and he was grinding it into his palm. Esther stood, sobbing hysterically, her head buried into her hands as she gasped for air.

Becky grabbed Tony by the arm and shook him. 'What are we going to do?' she demanded.

Tony pulled out of his trance. 'There is nothing to connect him to us. Nobody knows he is up here or why he came. Nobody knows about you and him. He won't have told anybody, and we certainly haven't.' He glared at the others and said loudly, 'That's right, ain't it? We're the only ones who know why he's here.'

'What are you saying?' asked Becky.

Tony said they should leave Palmer in the hut. There was nothing they could do to save him now. His body would not be found until the next day. There is no reason why anyone would connect them with his death but if anyone did ask them what they had been doing on the night he died they should say they had been up in the hut earlier in the evening but that they had left before it got dark and had spent the rest of the night on the beach. That would explain anything that linked them to the hut. They should also leave some of their stuff down on the beach as evidence they had been there.

'We can't just leave him here,' said Becky.

'Have you got a better idea?' demanded Tony. 'He's dead, Becky. There is nothing we can do about that now. There is no point in us getting the blame for this. The man had a heart attack. We didn't kill him. He would probably have had one anyway.' He grabbed Becky to steady her. 'It's not our fault, Becky. What we need to do now is stick to the same story. If we do that, they can't pin anything on us.'

Tony made the others promise they would stick to the story if they were asked about what had happened on that night. He kept saying there was nothing to connect them with Palmer. Esther and Stuart were still in shock and just agreed blankly with what Tony was saying. Only Becky remained doubtful.

'It's the only way, Becky,' said Tony. 'We could all go to prison otherwise. They'd make out we killed him, that we were accessories to murder.' He looked over at Esther. 'All of us, Becky. You wouldn't want that, would you? Think what it would do. Our lives would be ruined. Esther's life would be destroyed.'

He told Becky to give him her phone. He went over to Palmer's body, bent down, and felt inside his jacket until he found Palmer's phone. He said he would throw them both in the sea and, if anyone asked, Becky should say had lost hers when they had been down on the beach. He would destroy any other things that might connect them to Palmer: the notes, the present he had given her, anything that could establish a relationship between them and the teacher.

'This will be our secret,' said Tony. 'Now let's get out of here.' He turned off the camping lights. As they were leaving, Becky turned. In the darkness, she could see the silhouette of Alistair Palmer's dead body on the floor. It was an image that would haunt her for the rest of her life.

6

'Simon!' came the voice through the cold, morning air. It was a cry for help. 'Simon!' it came again, this time even more urgently. The shrill voice carried over the dunes. Simon had just put down the rucksack and was standing on the edge of the cliffs, peering out at the North Sea. He swivelled round. It was mistier inland and, at first, he could not locate where his wife's voice was coming from. He looked back, down the path they had come along from Sea Palling. Then he looked in the direction they were heading. The place was barren and deserted and Simon thought that maybe his wife had twisted her ankle and was lying in one of the hollows in the dunes. Then he realised she was calling from an old, abandoned shack a couple of hundred feet away. When he got there, his wife was standing outside. The door to the cabin was open behind her. She was shaking violently. 'There's a body inside,' she screamed. 'A dead body.'

Sandra Palmer knew something terrible had happened as soon as she saw the police car parked in front of the house. She had got the half-past-ten train from Norwich and it was nearly midday by the time the taxi dropped her and the children back in Homerton. The sky was threatening rain as they turned into the street which was empty except for the police car.

The babies had been fractious all the way from Acle and several times the taxi driver had looked at her in the rear-view mirror as if to say "can't you take care of your bleeding kids?". Sandra was flustered as she bundled the children and all their equipment out of the taxi, paid the driver and stood on the pavement putting up the double buggy.

The two police officers got out of the car, a man and a woman, and came along the road towards her. Sandra thought, for some reason, that there was always a woman officer present when bad news was delivered.

'Mrs Palmer, Mrs Sandra Palmer?' said the male officer. 'We would like to talk to you about your husband.' With practised ease he reached out and caught her elbow to steady her. He guided her towards the front door of the house. 'If we could just go inside.'

The woman officer took control of the buggy and the babies and swept up the bags. Sandra Palmer fumbled in her handbag for the keys and, with a shaking hand, opened the door.

'I'm afraid it's bad news,' said the policeman as soon as they were inside. 'You may need to sit down. We have found the body of a man we believe to be your husband.' He looked down at his notebook. 'A Mr Alistair Palmer.'

The police explained that, earlier that morning, the dead body of a man had been found in an abandoned cabin up on the cliffs. It looked as if he had suffered a fatal heart attack. From the documents found on the body, they were sure it was Alistair Palmer. The police said they would make arrangements for Mrs Palmer to formally identify the body and that they might need to ask her some questions later. Sandra Palmer was in shock. All that registered was that the body had been found in the old hut and she kept asking, 'Why would he be up there?'

After fifteen minutes, the police got up to leave. 'Is there anyone you can stay with?' asked the policewoman. 'Anyone who can come in and sit with you or maybe look after the children. You've had a terrible shock.' Sandra looked bemused. Why was this kind lady asking her to leave her home?

'I've got to wait for my husband,' said Sandra.

The policewoman patted her hand. 'It will take time to sink in,' she said.

'By the way,' said the policeman, 'where did your husband keep his phone? I assume he did have one. It's just that we couldn't find it on him.'

Sandra muttered something about the table in the hallway and the policeman went to look but there was nothing there.

*

The police were suspicious about the way Alistair Palmer had died. The pathologist confirmed it was a heart attack that had killed him, but that did not explain why he was in the old fisherman's hut on the cliffs or why he had gone there at night. It could be that he had arranged to meet someone there, somebody he wanted to meet in secret, or he could just have gone into the hut to explore it when he was out on a walk or to get out of the weather. There was no sign of a struggle and he had not been robbed – there was twenty pounds in his wallet as well as his bank cards. The only thing that seemed to be missing was his phone. This was the main thing that made the police suspicious.

Mrs Haylett came forward to tell the police she had seen Palmer in the town before he died and that he had told her he was going for a walk up on the cliffs. She said his breath smelt of whisky. The police asked around Homerton. Apart from a couple of people in the pub, no one else had seen him that night. They interviewed his fellow teachers and they spoke to his students, but nobody could shed any light on why he might have been in the hut on that night. Becky and Esther stuck to the story about them being on the beach.

The police asked Sandra Palmer all about her husband. They asked whether he had any debts, about who is friends and enemies were. They asked about his drinking, whether he had any other bad habits. Sandra said that Alistair had been under a lot of stress. That he was finding the workload difficult and there had been discipline problems with some of the kids. He had even been to the doctor to see if there was something that could help him sleep. She had no idea why he would have gone to the cabin on the night he died.

Peter Sullivan heard about Mr Palmer's death in the Fisherman's Return. It was the day his body was found. When Becky had got home the night before, he had asked where she had been. She said she had been down on the beach. She seemed a bit upset and clearly did not want to talk about things. Peter had thought nothing of it, but now he could not get the idea out of head that his beloved daughter was somehow involved in the teacher's death. He hated himself for thinking such disloyal thoughts, but it was hunch that he could not shake off. He knew that if Becky was involved, he would have to protect her. He had not always been a good father, and this was the one thing he could do to show her how much he cared.

It was one of the regulars at the garage who had told James Larner that Alistair Palmer was dead. 'It was a heart attack apparently. A couple of walkers found his body this morning. Someone told me a fox had got at it during the night, but I don't know if that's true.' James rushed upstairs and was sick in the loo. Whether he liked it or not, he was responsible for Palmer's death. If he had said something the night before, Palmer would still be alive now.

That evening, the five of them drove up in silence to Markers Ridge in Tony's car. They passed a bottle of vodka between them but none of them were drunk. The sun went down, staining the sky like a bloody wound. Tony turned the engine off and they sat there watching the lights of Homerton come on below as the twilight moved from mauve to purple. A silky voice was on the radio then the heartbreaking tug of Bob Marley singing "The Redemption Song".

'We are together on this, aren't we?' demanded Tony. 'If one of us caves, we are all for it. This is just between us. Nobody else can ever know.'

The police decided there was no point in investigating Alistair Palmer's death any further. There was no evidence that a crime had been committed. There was nothing to suggest anyone else was involved. But that did not stop the gossip from starting. Stories started to circulate around Homerton. There had been rumours before about Becky and some of the teachers. There is always someone in a school who has seen or heard something, and kids love to talk. Becky was always flirting with the male teachers and the young male teachers in the college could not resist talking about the girls they fancied, even if it was just banter. There had even been graffiti in the boys' loos that said "Becky fucks teachers". Several people claimed to have seen Becky and Tony and the others up on the cliffs on the night the teacher died, and everybody knew that Tony Fletcher was trouble.

Rumours spread all over town like a poisonous gas. It was all anybody talked about. Although Alistair Palmer had only been at the school for a couple of years, they talked as if he had been there for generations. 'He was a good teacher,' they said. 'My kids loved him. He was so kind and patient.'

In the staffroom, the male teachers were unusually quiet. They had heard the rumours about Becky and some of them had to admit that they too would have been tempted if a girl like her came on to them. It would have been difficult to resist.

It was the sort of opportunity that might make you throw caution to the wind; might make you do something stupid. 'There for the grace of God,' they muttered. They were already associating Becky with Alistair Palmer though they had no evidence of any relationship. They thanked their lucky stars that Becky had not chosen them, but a tiny bit of themselves secretly wished she had.

*

Becky Sullivan waited at the cottage window for the taxi that was coming to take her to her mother's house in Norwich. She had a suitcase at her feet and a holdall on the chair beside her. Everyone said it was for the best, her leaving Homerton to go and live with her mother. The rumours had just got too much. She could go to college in Norwich and resume her A levels. Her dad had suggested it, then he had second thoughts, but now he reluctantly agreed she would be able to start afresh in Norwich. It would be a clean slate. It was far enough away from Homerton, but not so far to feel as if she was being exiled to the other side of the country. With time and distance, she would be able to put the past few awful weeks behind her. She could begin life again.

Becky guessed it was for the best as well. The people in the town did not like having their neat little lives upset and Alistair Palmer's death had upset things big time. People were already avoiding her, and it was clear she made them uncomfortable. People had taken against her and would whisper hateful things behind her back. Becky would miss her friends, but they had their own problems to contend with. Esther's parents had told her to have nothing more to do with Becky and had taken her out of school. That had not stopped them meeting up a couple of times, but it was difficult to meet in secret in a small place like Homerton. Esther would not be able to finish her A levels now and would have to get a job. It already felt as if doors were closing on her life.

James and Stuart tried to pretend nothing had happened, but they were scared, and they knew things could never go back to what they were.

Even Tony thought it was a good idea for Becky to get out of town. He promised to visit her in Norwich, but she knew it was an empty promise and that he had said it just to make it easier for her to leave.

Becky looked across at the Fisherman's Return. Her dad had gone there for a drink saying he would be back to say goodbye, but he had been there for over an hour. She knew he would not want to face saying goodbye to his daughter and that he could not bear losing the only thing he loved. He would leave it until the last minute, until after the taxi had arrived and the whole sorry business could be rushed before the tears started. She knew that he would spend the whole evening drinking away his sadness.

Becky sensed somebody coming up the path towards the cottage, but it was not her dad, it was James. She went to meet him at the door. He looked awkward.

'This is a nice surprise,' said Becky.

'I thought I had missed you.' He wanted to say something but could not find the words.

Becky helped him. 'What is it, James?'

'It's my dad. I think he has got something going on with your mum.'

'What do you mean?' asked Becky, puzzled.

'He's been seeing her, in Norwich. Apparently it has been going on for months.'

'You are kidding, right?'

'I'm afraid not. I wish I was, Becks. It seems you might end up seeing more of my dad than I do.'

7

Becky's Return

The car stopped, grumbling at a crossroads, and Viktor leaned forward into the dashboard muttering "shit" and "crap" as the wipers swept aside the gusts of rain. He threw up his hands and said, 'What sort of a summer do they call this, eh?' Across the top of the windscreen was "Ace Taxis" written in reverse. On the dashboard, a phone in a holder showed Google Maps. There was a scattering of boiled sweets, an open packet of cigarettes and a can of energy drink. The song from *Midnight Cowboy* was playing faintly on the car radio.

The car pulled away sending a torrent of water against the windows. Viktor looked in the rear-view mirror at the young woman slouched on the back seat. She was in her mid-twenties. A jungle of black hair almost obscured her face, but you could still make out the thick eyebrows, the ink-pool eyes and the red lipstick on her slightly open mouth. Her eyes were closed but she was awake, and she twisted on the seat trying to get comfortable. She was not dressed for a weekend in the country. She was wearing a short, shiny black skirt and a sports vest. A leather jacket hung over her bare shoulders. Viktor sniffed a couple of times to pick up her perfume. He puckered his lips like a starving man with his face pressed against a restaurant window.

Becky Sullivan opened her eyes and yawned. She caught Viktor's gaze in the mirror and smiled. He lowered his eyes and leaned once more into the dashboard, his hands gripping the steering wheel. It was on nights like this that he hated being a taxi driver and he yearned to be back in Poland. It rained there too, of course, but at least it was his rain. The wipers swished furiously from side to side and the car's headlights cut through the slashing rain which sparkled on the windscreen.

'You live out this way then? You don't look like the sort of woman who'd live in a place like this.' He looked in the mirror, hoping to catch her eye.

'Oh God, no.' She checked herself. 'I did once. Live here, I mean. But it was a long time ago. I was just a girl.'

'You live up in London now then? In the big smoke. You look like a city girl.'

'And what does a city girl look like?' She was glad he had not taken her for a local.

'You know, a smart woman like you. You dress like a Londoner, trendy like. You have a sophistication about you. Like you have lived a bit.'

'I'm not sure that's the most flattering chat-up line.' She smiled.

Viktor blushed. After a moment he said, 'I suppose you've come back for a holiday then?'

She did not look like the sort of person who holidayed in Norfolk either and when he had picked her up at Great Yarmouth station from the last London train, he noticed she had no luggage with her.

'It definitely won't be a holiday. I have got some business I have to sort out, some loose ends that need tying up.' She made

49

her hand into a fist and moved back into the seat, indicating that the conversation was over. She had done her share of being nice to taxi drivers. Becky glanced down at her phone; there were hundreds of messages and new ones pinged in every second.

On the rear of the front seat was a red no-smoking sign. Becky bent over and fished out a packet of cigarettes from a huge handbag that lay at her feet. She glanced at Viktor in the mirror and nodded towards the cigarettes on the dashboard.

'You don't mind, do you?' She did not wait for an answer. Men always agreed with what she wanted. She could twist them round her fingers and had done so ever since she was a little girl. She could tell from the way Viktor chewed his bottom lip and kept glancing back at her that he was attracted to her. Most men were. He would be complicit in anything she did.

She lit the cigarette with a shaky hand then opened the back window and turned to blow the smoke out of it. She took a deep breath. Then she picked up her phone and tossed it out of the window.

'Hey. What are you…' Viktor stopped himself for a second time. After all, she was a good fare on a wet Wednesday evening, and he would prefer to look at her than any other customer. 'We all want to do that sometimes, eh?' He winked and smiled at her in the mirror.

Viktor turned up the radio and music filled the car. Becky relaxed. She had escaped from London and that was the main thing. No one would find her out here and she could lie low for a couple of weeks until things in London settled down. She was not expecting a warm welcome in Homerton and knew that dealing with what had happened in her hometown five years before would be difficult, but it would be no worse than the mess she had left behind in London.

Homerton appeared through the wipers of the car. A tall

sign loomed up with a painted scene of a yellow beach, blue skies and white seagulls and *Welcome to Homerton-On-Sea*.

Homerton was a nothing little place, too big to be a village and too small to be a town. On winter evenings, it seemed to disappear into the fog and on bright days you could take it all in with a simple turn of the head. It looked pretty in the sunshine and dreary in the rain. Bland modern houses had sprung up on the outskirts of the town and spread into the flat countryside beyond, but in the old town the years had buried the ancient cottages half into the ground. It was not the sort of place where someone like Viktor would feel welcome.

The taxi passed St Mary's Church and Larner's Garage and a neat village green with a stone cross in the middle and a pond in which a shopping trolley had been dumped. The streets were empty, and the houses were in darkness and several of them had For Sale signs tottering in the front gardens. The light of the telephone box next to the green flickered on and off. Outside the little supermarket, a board advertising the local newspaper read: *Another cat found strangled*. The illuminated clock on the old Methodist chapel showed it was five-past ten.

'They must go to bed early round here,' said Viktor.

'There is nothing else to do,' said Becky as the passing town dissolved in the rain.

The taxi turned into the Harbour Road. The pub was a pool of light in the darkness, a row of bright windows at street level, a string of lanterns swaying outside. Across the front in gold letters it said Fisherman's Return. A pub sign showed a trawler ploughing through heavy waves and it swung, creaking, in the rain.

There were a dozen men in the pub, and they all knew each other. The barmaid called them by their first names and poured their drinks without asking. There was the mumble of conversation. The evening was drawing to a close.

Stuart Bushell lent against the bar. His round face was covered in freckles. He was standing with James Larner.

The taxi's headlights passed the pub windows. Stuart turned and listened for the sound of the tyres crunching on the gravel drive a hundred metres away. He looked like he was sizing up a difficult problem.

'I reckon that will be her,' he said.

'You can't be sure,' said James. His neck went in and out like a chicken's. 'Just because Tony says she's coming back, it don't mean she is. He's full of bullshit.'

'I tell you; he knows the estate agent and the agent told him she was coming back to sell the house. We all knew she would be back one day. We knew, didn't we?' Stuart was not a man who liked to be questioned.

'She didn't even bother to come back for her own father's funeral. Why would she bother now? It's been six years. She could easily have got somebody else to sell the house for her.'

James went over to the window. For a few moments, he just stood there with his back to the bar.

'Well?' demanded Stuart.

'It's Becky alright. I'd know her anywhere. You had better call Tony.'

The taxi came to a halt in front of a flint cottage that was in a state of some disrepair. The engine purred as Becky got out. She leaned into the front window of the cab and quickly paid the driver. The taxi pulled away and she stood there for a moment in the rain, looking over at the pub as if trying to remember where she had seen it before. Then she turned and went inside the cottage.

The barmaid at the Fisherman's Return was calling time and picking up the empty glasses with the fingers of her right hand and wiping down the tabletops with her left.

'Come on, you two. It is way past eleven.' She looked at

the nearly full pints and shot glasses lined up on the bar. 'You'd think this was your bleeding home the amount of time you two spend here. Haven't you got someone to go back to?'

She knew they didn't. Since his dad had run off with Becky's mum, James lived alone with his brother Nick above the garage that he struggled to keep going. Stuart was single, though he was in an on/off relationship with his pregnant girlfriend Samantha Haylett.

James was twitchy despite the amount he had drunk. He had been that way since Palmer's death, which meant he had been that way for the whole of his adult life. He leaned in and hissed into Stuart's ear, 'Now she's back... Jesus, what are we going to do? It will just drag everything up again.'

'Pull yourself together,' said Stuart. 'You don't know nothing. She won't be around for long. I bet you that.'

The barmaid flicked the lights off and back on. 'I won't tell you two again, please piss off home.'

*

The grandfather clock in the hallway of the cottage showed it was half-past-eleven. A patch of light spread out from the room next door and there came the sound of Van Morrison singing "Tupelo Honey".

The front room was cluttered with faded, worn-out furniture. Old-fashioned wallpaper peeled from the walls. Books and piles of newspapers filled the corners. It was an old man's house that had not been decorated in years. On the mantelpiece were photographs of Becky's father leering drunkenly at the camera at various times in his life and there was a single, close-up photograph of Becky when she was a girl.

In the middle of the room, Becky was dancing by herself. She was barefoot, her arms raised above her head, a tumbler of

53

whiskey in one hand. Her eyes were closed, and she was lost within herself. She was a good dancer. Her hair tossed from side to side, her hips swung rhythmically to the music.

The music was so loud she did not hear the crackling of shoes along the gravel drive and the furtive voices outside the cottage.

Suddenly, there was a loud shattering sound and a brick smashed through the front window. Fragments of glass scattered across the floor. Becky was not shaken by what happened. She did not run to the window to catch sight of the perpetrator. She knew there were plenty of people in the town who did not want to see her return and some who hated her so much they would be happy to use a little violence to see her gone again.

Becky placed her drink on the table. She heard footsteps hurrying away. She bent down and picked up the brick and cut her finger on a shard of glass. She raised the finger to her lips, sucking the blood from it. Around the brick was wrapped a piece of paper on which were written the words: *Leave, you bitch.*

Becky took her finger from her mouth and started to laugh, tipping her head back and saying to herself, 'Welcome home, Becky. Welcome fucking home.'

8

There was the sound of activity outside the cottage; of things being lifted and hauled over the gravel and workers' voices. Becky raised herself on the bed and looked around the room where she had grown up. It seemed strange at first, then, as she blinked, completely familiar. The sounds coming through the window behind her head reminded her of the call she had made just after midnight to the number pinned on the board in the kitchen.

Becky stood up and stretched, worried for a second whether the curtains were open but decided she did not care. She had forgotten how small the rooms were in the cottage. Nothing had been touched since the day she had left. The same posters on the wall, her old clothes in the wardrobe, even the same duvet. It was as if her father had sealed the room on the day she had departed. Becky shook herself, as if trying to shed the memory. She checked her face in the mirror, and it was the face of a little girl preparing for her first day at school, the face of a teenager before her first party, the face of a young woman about to leave house where she grew up for the first time. Becky lifted the latch on the bedroom door and went padding towards the bathroom.

A van was parked on the green in front of the cottage. On the side of the van in red and gold letters its said *Haylett and*

Sons, Builders. A fine silver mist of rain fell from the sky. A creamy-coloured Labrador lay under the van, its round brown eyes watching as a young man – Jason Haylett – took a box of tools from the back of the van and crunched over the gravel to the cottage. He opened the little picket gate with a squeak and walked, whistling, up the overgrown path to the front window where his father, Sandy Haylett, was tapping out the shattered glass from the window frame.

'Didn't take long, did it?' whispered Sandy as he chewed on a splinter of wood. 'I knew the minute she came back there would be trouble.'

'Who do you think it was?' asked Jason, nodding towards the broken window.

'It could have been anyone. There are plenty round here who don't want to be reminded of the past. Some things are best forgotten. The problem is, with her back, it will all be raked up again.'

From somewhere inside the cottage came a sudden loud blast of the Beach Boys singing "Good Vibrations".

Sandy raised his eyebrows and sighed. 'She don't help herself, does she?'

A few moments later, Becky appeared wearing a short silk kimono that was tied loosely at the waist. Her hair flopped over her face in a dishevelled mess. She was carrying a tray on which were two mugs of tea.

'Morning,' she said breezily. 'I thought you might want a drink to get you started. I am really grateful for you coming round so quickly.' She smiled at Sandy. 'Sorry to wake you in the middle of the night.'

'That's ok. Your dad was a mate of mine. He wouldn't want his Becky alone in the cottage with a broken window.' Sandy looked at her kindly. 'It was tragic the way your dad died, it really was. Only the third person this century to be killed by an adder bite. Still, I guess it was an unusual way to go. Pete would have loved that. I can just see him down the pub telling the story now. He was a great one for his stories, was Pete.'

'And the pub,' said Becky.

Sandy laughed. He took a mug from the tray and nudged Jason, who was staring at the hint of Becky's breasts that peeked from beneath the kimono.

'Take your drink then, Jason lad,' he said.

Becky winked at Jason. 'I remember you,' she said. 'You used to get the same bus to school in Hemsby. You were in the lower school. You had an older sister, didn't you?'

'Still do.'

'Sam, wasn't it? She was a couple of years below me.'

Sandy cut in. 'Well, we must be getting on. It should only take us an hour or so. We'll call it a straight hundred for the window and the fitting. Cash if you've got it.' He finished the last of his tea and put the mug back on the tray. 'Go and get me the putty, Jason. The sooner we are finished here the better. I am sure Miss Sullivan has got a lot of things she has to get on with.'

*

Homerton was about half a mile from the sea. In between was a wide grassy area known as the staithes. This valley was dotted with wind-beaten shrubs, spiky trees and gorse topped hillocks. In amongst the grass and gorse lived adders, rabbits and lizards. The staithes ran from Sea Palling five miles in the north to Hemsby a couple of miles to the south. On the coastal side of the staithes, sand dunes climbed to a low rock- and grass-covered cliff that was slowly tumbling on to the wide beach below. A couple of hundred years ago, the staithes had been under water, forming a natural harbour between the cliffs and the town which enabled it to thrive as a fishing port. A single-track road ran from the town to a car park at the foot of the cliffs. Becky looked down the road and knew she would have to face it at some stage.

Becky decided to walk down to the beach. The morning mist had blown away and heaps of smudgy white clouds rolled across a blue sky. She had not been down to the beach in years and was forcing herself to go there. She had to face up to it sometime if she was going to move on.

As she crossed the staithes, she grew anxious. Her palms became clammy, and her stomach knotted. Her chest tightened. The cliffs were deserted. Empty cans and chip wrappers blew around the scrubby bushes. Seagulls circled and dived overhead. The fisherman's hut was still there. Becky stood in front of it. Broken glass crunched beneath her feet. The door was falling open, but she could not go in. She closed her eyes and pictured the face of Mr Palmer, crying like a child.

Becky felt dizzy and steadied herself against the damp wall of the hut. Her stomach squeezed into a fist, and she bent over as a spasm gripped her gut and a stream of acid bile sprayed on to the ground. She glanced down at the pool of vomit, wiped her mouth with the back of her hand, then turned and headed quickly back towards the town.

What she needed now was a decent cup of coffee. There had been a tearoom in Homerton for as long as people could remember. It was a small place with eight tables inside and half a dozen in the courtyard garden behind. It sold sandwiches and cakes but also English breakfasts and chips.

A bell tinkled as you pushed open the sticky front door causing the other customers to stop mid-forkful to see who had entered. When Becky stepped into the café the dozen or so customers stopped eating and talking. Everyone looked at her and a palpable tension descended on the room. One old man tutted and shook his head. A woman mumbled, 'Shame.' Someone dropped a spoon on the floor with a clang. People shifted in their chairs and averted their eyes as Becky walked breezily to the counter.

'Esther!' said Becky. 'My God, I didn't know you worked here.' She reached out her hand to one of the women behind the counter. Then, seeing that the women was clearly agitated by her sudden appearance, let it fall.

Esther was shorter and more petite than Becky, with blonde hair that was pulled back into a tight bun. She had large blue eyes and a pink complexion that glowed with a sheen of sweat from the heat of the kitchen.

Esther looked embarrassed. She twisted her hands in her apron and rubbed a foot behind her leg. The other woman behind the counter was glaring at her. Esther and Becky had not spoken to each other for several years. Esther had visited her in London once for her twenty-first birthday, but things had been awkward and tense, and Esther had returned home early.

'I heard you were back,' said Esther, almost whispering.

'Did you? News travels fast. It's great to see you again.'

Everyone in the tearoom was looking towards the counter. Esther peered over Becky's shoulder and said, 'Perhaps it is best if you sit outside, you know what they are like around here. I'll bring you a coffee. I've got my break in ten minutes, and we can talk then.'

'Of course. Look, I will see you in a minute. It's too stuffy in here anyhow.' Becky went towards the glass doors that led out on to the courtyard. She turned and poked out her tongue to the other customers.

It was warm and sheltered in the courtyard. Becky lit a cigarette and drew in deeply. After a few minutes, Esther came out. She put down two mugs of coffee on the table.

'I never thought you would come back,' Esther said. She accepted a cigarette and let Becky light it.

'I need to sell the cottage. Besides, I wanted a break from London. Things are a bit tricky there.'

'Are you going to stay long?'

'A few weeks maybe. I get the impression people would prefer it to be a short as possible.'

'What did you expect, Becky? Things don't get forgotten easily in a place like this. You know that.' Esther blew a stream of smoke into the air. 'You know I'm married to Tony, don't you?' She watched Becky's face for a reaction.

'I heard. You didn't send me an invite to the wedding.'

'I didn't have your address. You never seemed to stay anywhere for more than a few weeks. Besides, it was all really quick. Not that we needed to get married in the end, as I lost the baby.'

'I'm sorry, I didn't know.' Becky rubbed Esther's arm. Esther explained that Tony had been relieved rather than devastated. He just wasn't the father type.

'What's Tony doing now? I didn't think he would stay around here.'

'Oh, this and that. You know Tony. In any other life he would have been a millionaire. I don't want to know what he does because I am sure I wouldn't like it. Let's just say it won't be legit.'

Esther stood up and drank the remains of her coffee. 'Look, I've got to go back in – that woman's a dragon.' She hesitated. 'It still eats me up sometimes; that night, I mean. I guess it's the same with all of us.' She took a last drag of the cigarette and stubbed it out. 'You coming back here isn't going to help, is it? You do realise that? Look, there's a day at the pub on Saturday, why don't you come to that? Tony will be there and Stuart and… Well… I'll leave it up to you.

But I'd like to see you again even if nobody else does.' Esther went back inside, and Becky watched her go. With her black skirt and white shirt, it was almost as if she was watching her schoolfriend in her uniform all those years ago.

9

St Mary's west tower could be seen from every house in the town. It was one of the finest churches in a county of great churches. Becky knew it well. She had been there for harvest festivals and carol services, for weddings and christenings. The church bells had tolled throughout her childhood.

After a meeting with the estate agent, Becky went to the church. She needed to visit the grave of her father. A sudden shower started as she reached the church and she dived under the lychgate for shelter. She sat on the worm-eaten wooden seat and looked out at the rain. On one of the timbers holding up the roof was carved BS/TF. She had forgotten: Becky Sullivan and Tony Fletcher. He had carved it with his penknife one dull Sunday evening when they first met.

The door of the church was locked. On it was pinned a sheet of paper that said: *Due to recent thefts from this church, it has become necessary to close the church when it is unoccupied.* Becky shook the metal ring handle of the door anyway, then she left the porch and walked around to the north side of the church.

She went past the gravestones of old sailors to the patch where the more recently deceased were buried. She knelt beside a white marble tombstone on which was carved:

In loving memory of Peter Sullivan
1952–2005
Father, husband, friend
He never missed his round

'Heartfelt,' muttered Becky cynically. She thought how they could have added "gambler, womaniser and drunk" to the epitaph but she regretted now not having returned for his funeral. She was an only child and her dad doted on her. He called her his "angel" and she could get out of him anything she wanted. But by the time he died, they had not seen each other for nearly three years, and they rarely spoke on the phone. Her life was in such a mess at the time that coming back for the funeral would have been impossible.

Only later did she find out the bizarre way in which her father had died. He had been on a bender and had stumbled into some bracken whilst wandering drunkenly in the staithes, disturbing an adder which had taken its revenge.

As she got up to leave, Becky glanced at the other graves, but she knew there was not one for Alistair Palmer. Although the days following his death had been a blur, she remembered his widow had insisted he be buried in his hometown.

Becky's mum had left when she was doing her GCSEs and had ended up living with Tom Larner in Norwich. Becky had gone to live with them after Palmer's death, but she hated Norwich and as soon as she reached eighteen she escaped to London. She had not seen James Larner for years.

Becky walked along the road from the church to the garage. The old sign above the forecourt read: *Larner Garage*, but there was a big gap between the two words, and you could still see where "and sons" has been scrubbed from the sign and painted over.

On the concourse, in front of the kiosk, sat a short man who looked no more than twenty with thin wispy hair. His legs just touched the concrete floor. He was deep in concentration and his lips moved as his fingers followed the story in the comic he was reading.

'Hello, Nick.'

He looked up at Becky and smiled.

'How have you been keeping?' She bent down and the man threw his chubby arms over her shoulders and hugged her.

'Becca?'

'That's right.'

'I missed you.' Though it was clear he was struggling to place the name in his memory. He could recall names from years back and things he had read and seen though he had no idea what they meant.

'Where's James?' she asked, and he nodded towards the garage and went back to his comic.

Next to the kiosk was an open workshop where the cars were repaired – you went through this to get to the flat above. It smelt of grease and petrol. Becky opened the side door and climbed the stairs. The smell of pot got stronger as she went up. At the top, she entered the open door of the flat to a fug of dope. James was sitting at the kitchen table smoking a massive joint. Cans of beer were piled in front of him. He was about to jump up then saw it was her.

'Working hard, I see.'

'I wondered how long it would be before you came around. Everyone knows you are back.' He passed her the joint. 'I guess you'll be needing some of this?'

The flat was a tip; dishes toppled in the sink, takeaway cartons were strewn around the kitchen, a heap of dirty clothes lay on the floor.

'Well, as we are practically related…' She took a drag and handed back the joint, cleared some car magazines from a chair and sat down. 'How've you been?'

'See for yourself,' said James, indicating the room with a sweep of his arm. 'The business is going to the wall, and I've got that imbecile downstairs to look after.' His hand shook as he lifted the can to his lips. 'And you? What became of the amazing Becky? I can't say I've seen you on the TV yet, so I guess they haven't gone quite as planned.'

Becky shrugged. 'I've been OK.'

James was agitated. His whole body twitched. His complexion was grey and scabby. He looked exhausted.

'Perhaps you've been smoking too much of that stuff.' Becky put her hand on his and patted it. She felt his hand tremble beneath hers.

'You still look good,' he said. He was leering at her, mentally undressing her.

Becky brushed away her fringe. She turned away.

James could smell the perfume on her neck, that long beautiful neck that he had dreamed of kissing at school. Then he thought of her and Tony. James reached out and touched Becky's neck, moving her hair to one side.

Becky tensed. 'Don't do that,' she said.

'I missed you, Becky. We all have.'

Becky leaned forward and kissed him on the forehead. 'Don't let the past get to you, James. It was a long time ago.'

'It's just with you coming back. It seems like yesterday.'

'Yesterday was never a good day,' said Becky, getting up to leave.

She left the garage and headed back to the cottage. James stood at the window of the flat and watched as she went. Some of his paranoia had rubbed off on her and she sensed the curtains twitch as she walked along the road and conversations fall silent as she passed people on the pavement. She decided to get out of Homerton again as soon as the arrangements on the cottage were settled.

She heard quick footsteps behind her and turned. There was a woman in her mid-thirties, with lank, greasy hair and a hard slash of a mouth. She was weighed down with bags – shopping bags in each hand and school bags tucked under her arms. She was wearing jeans and a lumpy sweatshirt. Two tousle-haired boys followed after her.

'Hey, you! I want a word with you.' She caught up with Becky and dropped her bags on the pavement. She yanked at Becky's arm, pulling her backwards. Close up, Becky could smell the sour drink on her breath.

'You little bitch,' she snarled. 'How dare you show your face around here again?' Flecks of spit hit Becky's face. The woman looked as if she about to cry and Becky realised it was Alistair Palmer's wife. She had aged considerably since Becky had last seen her.

The two boys looked up at their mother, but she shook them off.

'I know what you did, you little tart. My husband is dead because of you.' She squeezed one of the boys to her side. The woman raised her arm to hit Becky, but she intercepted it. 'You knew exactly what you were doing,' said the woman. 'You scheming bitch.' Suddenly she gave a little sob. Her hands were shaking.

Becky thought she might collapse on the road. She reached out and steadied the woman's elbows. She picked up the bags and handed them to the woman. 'I'm sorry. I mean that.'

10

It was just after eight in the morning and the sun was trying to push its way through the grey clouds.

'I can't do it; I just can't do it.' Sandy Haylett flumped down on the bench as if every emotion had been wrung out of him. His head was shaking from side to side with incredulity. His huge body trembled with grief. He buried his head into his thick meaty hands. 'Who would do such a thing?' he sobbed.

'Come on, Dad,' said Jason, putting his arm around him. 'Let's get the poor thing down.'

Sandy blew his nose. 'I couldn't believe it when Mrs Tremlett phoned. What sort of sick bastard would go round doing such a thing,' said Mr Haylett in disbelief.

'I know, Dad. It's evil, that's what it is.'

Sandy looked up at the dead cat that had been flung over the sign welcoming people to Homerton. The cat's body was flopped lifelessly over the cross, its paws dangling in the air. Its eyes stared at the patch of scrubby grass that lay below. 'It's like he's been crucified up there. If I ever catch the bastard who did this, I'll kill him.' He ground his right fist into his left hand. 'What am I going to tell your mother and sister?'

Jason went and pulled the ladder off the roof of the van

and brought it over the green. He placed a ladder against the sign and tested it. 'I'll lift him down. I guess we had better report it to the police.'

'Nothing they can do. They're bleeding useless. I doubt they're going to get off their fat arses for something like this. No, I reckon this is one we'll have to sort out.'

'What do you mean?'

'Nobody does this to my cat and gets away with it. I'll string them up from the cross myself.'

'Still, we should take him to the vet.' Jason climbed the first couple of steps of the ladder.

'I just want to get him down. Hurry up, lad. The sooner we get him down the sooner we can get him away from prying eyes.' Jason climbed a couple more steps up the ladder and started to lift the dead cat off the sign. He wrapped the body in the decorator's sheet and carried it over to the van.

*

Becky stood on the other side of the road from the Fisherman's Return, hesitating about whether to go in. Across the railings in front of the pub was a banner which had come lose at one corner and which said: *Fun Day – This Saturday*. There was the faint smell of barbecue in the air and the noise of children. Becky could just see the red top of the inflatable slide in the pub garden. Her hands were stuffed into the pockets of her jeans. She was not sure that she wanted to meet the others again, but she needed a drink and wanted company. She took a deep breath and crossed the road.

When Becky entered the low-ceilinged bar of the Fisherman's Return, she sensed the hostility. There were about thirty people in the pub, sitting and standing at the bar and gathered round tables. Faces turned in her direction as she pushed open the wooden door and stumbled on the step inside. The conversation fell to a whisper as people realised who it was, and they turned away.

Becky could see James and Stuart sitting at a table in a far corner of the bar. There were two others with their backs to her – one she recognised as Esther and the other one she guessed was Tony. She gave a half-hearted wave at James, and he beckoned her over.

'You came,' he said as she reached the table. He pushed his chair back and stood up. 'Come on, sit here. I'll get you a drink. What do you want?'

Becky nervously acknowledged the others on the table. 'I'll have a gin and tonic,' she said. 'A double.'

On the table there was an awkward silence at first but then Esther said that she was glad she had come, and Stuart made a joke about her having been in the loo for five years and they were just deciding whether to check if she was ok. Becky glared at Tony as if to force him to acknowledge her and Esther nudged him, and he said, 'Welcome back. The place hasn't been the same without you.' She sensed the old sneer in his voice, but his smile was generous.

Stuart brought the drinks over and sat opposite Becky, with Tony and Esther on one side and James on the other. They had the glassy-eyed look of those who'd had a few drinks but who now wanted to be on their best behaviour.

Soon things relaxed and they started to laugh and joke – except for Esther who sat with her lips firmly and grimly pressed together as if she was frightened that to let them part would reveal a set of rotten teeth. Esther, who was always the kind one, the one who would talk sweetly from their meeting at the bus stop in the morning to their goodbye at the bus stop in the late afternoon. Becky tried to cheer her up, but something was making her tense and moody.

'Come on,' said Becky, 'let's go and get some fresh air. I'm sure the boys can live without us for a few minutes.'

Becky took a cigarette from Esther. 'What's wrong with you two?' she asked. 'You can feel the tension in there.'

'He's drinking too much,' said Esther. 'He's ok now but it won't stay that way. I know what he's like when he's had a drink.'

When Becky and Esther came back, Esther looked more relaxed. For the next hour as they sat drinking, the three men vied for Becky's attention, ignoring Esther. Everyone drank too much and did not care. Even Esther had decided that the only option was to drink. It was as if there was a collective desire amongst all those present in the Fisherman's Return that afternoon to get blind drunk; the success of the day being judged solely on whether it could be obliterated by alcohol.

There was the jingle of bells and the clip-clop of shoes crossing the pub's stone floor. Two men in white trousers and shirts went up to the bar. They both had beards and they were trussed up with ribbons and sashes and belts. One had a concertina slung over his back. They were carrying four pewter tankards, which they banged down on the bar.

'Fill these up with ale, landlord, and we'll get started.' When he smiled you could see his teeth were all crooked.

The other man wiped the sweat from his forehead with a handkerchief then took off his spectacles and wiped those. He said, 'If we're lucky we'll be over and done before the rain comes in.'

'Ladies and gentlemen,' bellowed a voice from behind the bar. 'The Hemsby Morris Men will be starting in five minutes. Out front in the car park.' There was a shuffling of chairs and a few people got up from their tables.

'Come on,' said Stuart. 'It'll be a laugh.' He took Becky's hand and pulled her up.

'You coming?' Becky asked Esther.

She glanced at Tony before standing up and saying, 'Of course.'

'I'd better go,' said James, finishing his drink.

'Ah, do you have to?' said Esther.

'I'd better,' said James. 'It's Nick. He gets a bit anxious if I leave him too long. He worries I won't come back.'

'Oh, let him go,' snapped Tony, scowling. 'You're used to leaving early, aren't you, James?'

By six o'clock, the afternoon had descended into a drunken stupor. Tony brought over a tray of shots and Stuart went over to the jukebox and fed it a dozen coins. 'Come on, let's dance,' he said.

'What?' Becky glanced over at Tony and saw him sneer. Esther noticed her seeking Tony's approval.

'Dance. It's ok. Nobody cares.' Stuart held out his hand and it hovered expectedly in the air.

'Don't be stupid,' said Becky. She sensed others in the pub looking at them like wedding guests waiting for a bride and grooms first dance. 'I'm too drunk.'

'All the better. Come on, it'll be fun.' Stuart's hand thrust a bit forward.

Becky looked up at Stuart's round beseeching face. *Fuck it*, she thought. It had been years since somebody had *wanted* to dance with her. She took his hand for a second time that afternoon and he pulled her up. 'My pleasure,' she said, giving a little curtsy.

'You're pathetic,' snarled Tony.

They started shuffling on the bit of floor in front of the table. At first, they shuffled awkwardly in front of each other, giggling. But then she pulled him towards her. She put her arms over his shoulders and clasped them behind his back. He held her hips. They were face to face. She could feel his hands tentatively on the small of her back and she rocked her buttocks from side to side then moved them forward so her crotch was pressed up against his.

She felt him stiffen against her as their feet found their rhythm and their hips moved together. Stuart could feel Becky's breasts under the fabric of her blouse, her breathing growing deeper, synchronising with his. She could sense Tony watching them. She wanted his attention, his jealously. It felt good that he was looking at her. She moved her hands up and ran them through Stuart's hair, leaned in and kissed him, smelling the beer on his breath. She felt his hands squeeze her bottom and his crotch rub against her. He pressed for another kiss, but Becky pulled away.

Tony had stood up and was pulling Esther after him. 'We're off,' Tony snapped.

Stuart turned and was about to ask them to stay for another one, but Becky whispered, 'I want you,' in his ear. Stuart looked incredulous. Becky kissed him again and once more he felt the plump slippery softness of her lips against his, then her teeth as she playfully bit his lower lip.

Tony turned at the door of the pub and stared at Becky, who was looking at him over Stuart's shoulder. She was smiling.

Just then a fat man came rolling from the bar towards the exit. He banged his shoulder against Becky, pushing Stuart to one side as he did so. 'You haven't changed, you little slut,' he snarled as he made for the door.

Outside, black storm clouds came rolling in from the North Sea. A can rattled along the pavement, the trees swayed and snapped in the wind. The funday banner had blown off and was throwing itself erratically around the car park.

The door of the pub was pushed open, and two figures appeared briefly silhouetted in the light from the bar. They ran across the road, hunched together under a coat.

Stuart and Becky stumbled into the kitchen. 'We'd better get out of these clothes. We're soaking,' said Becky.

Stuart steadied himself against the side of the kitchen. The room was spinning, and he looked down at his feet to focus on something near. He regretted now having drunk so much.

Becky tossed the wet coat on to the kitchen table and clumsily pulled off her shoes. She was barefoot. 'Can you undo these for me,' said Becky lowering her chin to the buttons of her blouse. 'My fingers are too wet.' The words were like an echo. At first, she could not place where she had heard them before, then with a shock she remembered that she had asked Mr Palmer to unbutton her school shirt on that night when she had seduced him after staying behind in school.

Now Stuart's fingers fumbled with the buttons just as his had done, the hot breath against her breastbone as he bent his head to focus on the fiddly task of pushing the tiny buttons through their holes, desperate to pull the blouse open but nervous about seeming incompetent. Becky remembered the white flecks of dandruff on top of Mr Palmer's head, how she thought his hair was badly combed, his breathing almost like a grunt as his thick fingers pinched at the cotton of her school blouse.

She could hear Stuart breathing too, a rasping breath. His fingers brushed against her breasts.

'Stop it,' she said abruptly. 'I'll do it. You're pissed.' She quickly unbuttoned her blouse and cast it aside. She unzipped her jeans and toppled out of them then she grabbed a towel and started to dry her hair. Stuart watched as she moved around the kitchen in her bra and knickers. She liked being watched. His eyes devoured her slender legs, her flat stomach, the small, firm breasts.

Becky dropped the towel and went over to Stuart. She rubbed her hands against his crotch. 'It doesn't mean anything. You know that, right?' He nodded. 'Come on, let's go upstairs.'

The bedroom was cold. Lying in bed, Becky could hear Stuart in the bathroom. She was getting impatient and already starting to regret the situation. She was sobering up and the drunken desire of earlier was starting to fade. Stuart no longer seemed attractive.

Stuart came naked out of the bathroom and ran to the bed. He was all eager desperation, his hands moving over Becky's body as if needing to touch every part of her. Becky wanted more than this boyish fumbling. His hands were clumsy and clammy. He was grabbing at her flesh. She put her hands between his legs, but he was flaccid. She moved her fingers delicately over his crotch, but nothing happened. Now she just wanted it over with. She grabbed him and pulled him on top of her, but it was no good.

'What's wrong?' she asked. 'Don't you want me?'

Stuart rolled on his back. His breathing subsided.

The light from the streetlamp outside illuminated Becky's sleepy face. Stuart had never lain beside such a beautiful face.

Becky turned and gently took his hand. 'I'm not a romantic,' she said quietly 'You don't need to pretend to love me, but I like you, Stuart, so be kind to me.' She moved his hand. 'Come on, let's try again.'

11

Stuart leaned in and stretched his face back into shape in the mirror. Becky lay on the bed, her naked body half covered by a duvet. Stuart watched her in the mirror, his gaze following the outlines of her body as she turned in the pale sunlight that seeped in through a gap in the curtains. Her skin was tanned except for her buttocks and breasts. Her hair washed against the pillow.

A rancid taste filled Stuart's mouth. He looked at his reflection with self-loathing. The freckles on his face seemed more pronounced than usual. No wonder women rejected him. He hated how he looked. He brushed his hair back with his hand, wanting to make himself more desirable. He felt ashamed by his failure to perform the night before. His one chance to have sex with Becky, the girl he had obsessed about since school, and he had blown it, just as he had failed at everything else in his sad little life.

Here he was at twenty-five, single, still living with his parents and working as a bus driver. Even the baby that Sam was having had been a mistake. He wasn't sure when or how it had happened, but it certainly had not been planned.

He looked at his round, pudgy face. He was like a clown. What a joke! Surely Becky had only wanted him because there was no one else and when she woke, he would see the horror on her face as she realised it was him – good old Stuart; the classroom fool, the sidekick, the dupe, the big fat tub.

But she had wanted him. She had said so, the words coming out of those lips just as he had dreamed it for years: 'I want you.'

If only he had been able to satisfy her. He felt an anger rise in him, an anger with himself but also with Becky. He looked at her in the mirror. She was so beautiful, and sexier than any woman he had ever seen, and God knows he had watched enough porn over the years to know what a sexy woman looked like. But she was dangerous too, always had been. Even at school there was something cruel and calculating about her. A cock teaser, a slag, flaunting herself at every opportunity, leading you on and then rejecting you. It was as if she wanted to use her body as a weapon.

In a small flat on the other side of Homerton, Esther was cooking Tony's breakfast. Lined up on the kitchen top was a row of cookery books which she would read but never cook from. Tony liked his food plain and familiar and they ate the same meals each week.

Esther wiped down the surface and placed on it the eggs and bread, the packets of smoked bacon and pork sausages. She was petite with a well-rounded figure, not plump (Tony didn't like fat women) but not skinny either (Tony didn't like scrawny women). She had a pretty, oval-shaped face with glowing olive skin and big cow-like eyes. A thin nose pointed to rosebud lips. She looked vaguely Mediterranean, though her family had lived in the area for generations.

A radio played jaunty pop music quietly enough so as not to disturb Tony, who was next door in what they called the dining room, but which was no more than a table and a couple of chairs at one end of the sitting room.

Tony and Esther had been a couple for the past four years and had got married two years ago. Her parents had put down the deposit on the flat as a wedding present and they managed to meet the mortgage through Esther's job at the café, her work as a teaching assistant at St Mary's Primary School and Tony's various wheeling and dealings. Esther knew that it was only a matter of time before Tony got caught and ended up in jail, but the prospect did not bother her. A normal job just would not cut it with him; he needed more money than it could provide and more quickly. He also liked the excitement.

Her life was the opposite of exciting. It felt to her that her best years had been at school and college with Becky. After the Palmer affair, she had given up college and never did her A levels. She got work and hung around, and eventually started going out with Tony. The months just passed by. Things were never the same after Becky left. Esther had settled for a life that she did not want but was too apathetic to do anything about.

She turned the sausages in the hot fat. She laid the three rashers of bacon next to the sausages in the frying pan, moving them back and forth with a spatula. She set the timer to ensure they were cooked for the correct amount of time. There had been times over the past couple of years when she had stood in the kitchen and seriously contemplated plunging her hands into hot fat just to make herself feel something. Something intense.

'You look like you're going to church,' said Tony, peering up from his phone when Esther brought in his breakfast on a tray.

He was tipped back on the chair, his arms and legs sprouting from his shorts and tee shirt. A tattoo of an eagle was emblazoned on his left bicep. Lying next to the chair was a scruffy lurcher that growled as Esther came in.

Esther placed Tony's breakfast in front of him. 'This will

set you up for the day,' she said, as if he was a customer at the café. She sat down opposite Tony. 'I saw you looking at Becky yesterday.'

'I don't know what you mean.'

'Yes you do. You were undressing her with your eyes.'

'You can't blame me. She's a sexy woman.'

'Don't.'

'Don't pretend you weren't looking at her as well. Everyone was. She was your schoolgirl crush.'

'You disgust me,' said Esther, standing up. Her face turned red.

*

At the Haylett's ramshackle house overlooking the sea, Mrs Haylett was sitting like a great ball of fluff on the settee in the living room. In her pudgy hands was a tub of ice cream which she kept spooning into her mouth with a satisfied sucking noise. The TV was on in the background, unwatched, and the smell of the Sunday roast cooking in the kitchen filled the air. The room was hot and stuffy.

'You're meant to eat that after dinner, not as a bloody starter,' said Sandy Haylett.

'Oh shut up, you miserable git.'

She turned to Samantha, who was wedged into one of the armchairs. 'I remember when I was pregnant with you. I had a craving for ice cream.'

'Pity it didn't stop when she was born,' said Sandy.

'Oh just ignore him,' said Mrs Haylett. 'He's a moody bugger.'

Sam was an oasis of calm in the daily chaos that surrounded her. She had been engaged to Stuart for nearly nine months, though she knew it was not his baby.

'Oh!' She gave a sharp intake of breath. 'Jesus, I think it's started,' she said.

'It can't be. You're not due for another month.' Mrs Haylett glared at her husband. 'This is you, this is. All that fuss over the bloody cat has made her premature.'

'It's not that, Mum. Babies can come early, you know that.' Sam felt another twinge and gave out a gasp.

'Bleeding Stuart,' said Jason. 'He's useless. He should be here at a time like this rather than cavorting around town.'

'He's probably working,' said Sandy. 'He wants this baby as much as she does.'

'Yeh well, you don't know what I know. I've got eyes. If that bastard doesn't do his duty…'

'Oh, shut up, Jason.' Sam gave a sharp intake of breath. 'It's definitely coming. Can you go and get my bag from the bedroom? And, Dad, can you phone Stuart? My phone is over there.'

Stuart was standing in the kitchen making coffee. He wanted to get his story straight before facing Samantha again. He was determined not to mess it up this time. Sam was a great girl. What he liked about her most was that she did not demand all that emotional stuff. She was not needy like the others. She was organised and practical and planned things out. That is not to say she was cold. Far from it. She was a good laugh and enjoyed going out. It is just that she did not overcomplicate things. Take the baby, for example. She did the classes and check-ups and all that, but she did not make a fuss and insist Stuart go with her. In fact, Stuart seemed keener on the whole thing than she did.

The smell of the coffee wafted up Stuart's nostrils. He listened as Becky came down the stairs. She was wearing her father's dressing gown. She came up behind Stuart and leaned over him, pressing her breasts against his back.

'You're still here,' she said.

Stuart turned around. 'I was making us coffee.'

'It smells good.'

She licked her bottom lip with her tongue and casually asked, 'Do you want to try again?' He felt her body against his chest.

'Do you really want me to?' he asked.

'Of course.' But she did not sound too enthusiastic.

Stuart was about to succumb when his phone rang, buzzing on the kitchen top. He bent down and raised it to his ear.

'Yes?'

'She is having the baby,' said Mr Haylett. 'We will meet you at the hospital. The Royal in Acle. You'd better get there pronto, boy. Don't let her down.'

12

By Wednesday, the two brief days of sunshine had gone, and the beach was empty again. It was four in the afternoon. From one end of the beach came two figures hunched against the wind and the rain. As they drew closer, you could see it was two women in long coats and wellington boots. Hats were planted firmly on their heads. They were walking a couple of small dogs.

'Oh, do come on, Penelope,' said one woman to the other.

'Don't be such a bully,' said Penelope. 'I am going as fast as I can. You know I've got bad feet.'

'You have town feet. If you had grown up in the country like I did you would be able to walk for miles, whatever the weather.'

Penelope pulled a face behind Laetitia's back. They reached a slipway at the end of the beach that went up to the top of the cliffs. Next to the slope were boulders that had been eroded from the cliff face and the remains of bungalows that had once sat on top of the cliff but had long since fallen to the sea. Penelope sat down on one of the rocks. She took off her left boot and rubbed her foot through the thick woollen sock. Laetitia joined her.

'You poor thing. When we get back to the cottage, I'll prepare you a steaming-hot foot bath and a good stiff drink.'

The dogs went off sniffing amongst the boulders. Laetitia took in a gust of air. She looked over lovingly at Penelope. 'Come on, let's get you back into the warmth.' She called out to the dogs. One of them was barking. 'What is it, you silly things?' said Laetitia going over to them.

Penelope was putting her boot back on when she heard a high-pitched yelp from Laetitia's direction. Laetitia stood with her hand at her mouth. She was staring at the body of a dead cat that had been flung between the rocks.

*

At around half-past-eleven, James woke suddenly and for a few moments he looked around in a daze, unable to place where he was. He had been dreaming he was in a wheelchair surrounded by the flashing lights of ambulances and police cars, and someone was slapping him across the face, pleading with him to stay awake and not lose consciousness. He was dreaming about his own end.

James saw Nick glaring at him from a chair opposite. He took in his surroundings, reorientating himself. A chat show was blaring out of the TV with laughter and applause. The smell of cold takeaway Chinese filled the room, the half-empty tinfoil containers piled up on the table. A tumbler of whiskey was on the floor next to where James was sitting, and as he stretched he knocked it over.

'You were snoring,' said Nick in his babyish voice. 'You've been asleep for over an hour. You sound like a pig. You said we would watch *Talent Quest* together.'

James's brain was throbbing inside his skull; his mouth was dry and rancid. His back ached from where he had been slouching awkwardly in the chair. The last thing he could remember was the weather forecast at the end of *News at Ten*.

'Did you just slap me?' asked James.

Nick pulled an incredulous face.

James felt at his feet for the glass, picked it up and stood, arching his back. He yawned.

'You drink too much,' accused Nick.

'Do I now?'

'Yes, every night.'

'Well so would you if you had my shit life.'

James went over to the table to pour another drink, but he decided not to. Nick looked wounded. He knew he was the reason why James stayed in Homerton. He knew because James kept telling him.

'I'm sorry. Do you want to watch *TQ* on catch up?'

'It's too late now. I'm tired.'

James said he would make Nick a cocoa and he went into the kitchen. He was in no mood for being made to feel guilty for missing a stupid programme. Sometimes it was too much. The demands kept coming from all sides and it felt like he had no control over his life, like in a film when someone is driving and they find the steering wheel does not work and the brakes don't work and the car is speeding towards the edge of a cliff.

He was struggling to keep the garage going and the truth was his heart was not in it. He was no good with the customers. He could not stand all that small-talk stuff, being polite and cheerful and pretending to like people just as he had pretended to like Tony for years when really he wanted to ring his neck.

Nick wasn't easy either. You could not leave him alone for more than a few hours and he was emotionally demanding. James knew Nick would only get worse as he grew older. James stirred the mug of cocoa and carried it through to Nick. He had run away from many things, but he was not going to run away from his brother.

After Nick had gone off to bed, James poured himself another whiskey. He went over to the window and looked out at the deserted town. He wondered if he would ever escape or whether he would still be standing there in twenty years' time, growing more lonely and bitter with each passing summer.

13

A car pulled up in front of the Haylett's house and Stuart got out. He quickly went around to the other side of the car and opened the passenger door. He helped Samantha out, fussing around her. She had a baby cradled in her arms. She bent down and kissed its forehead then nodded towards the back seat, telling Stuart to bring the bags.

Mr and Mrs Haylett were waiting at the door. They started down the path to meet Sam and the baby.

Jason watched the scene from an upstairs window, thinking that now Sam would get even more of their attention. He looked at Stuart with contempt. It disgusted him that Stuart was the father of his sister's baby.

As Samantha got to the gate, Tony stepped in front of her and she jumped in surprise. She had not noticed him hanging around a bit further along the road. 'What are you doing here?'

'Let's have a look then,' said Tony. He poked his head towards her chest and fingered the baby's shawl down a little bit to reveal more of its face, half of which was covered with a red mark.

'It's a boy,' said Samantha, quickly covering up the face again.

'Pity,' sniffed Tony. 'What's that mark?'

'They say it'll go in a few days. It's just the way he came out.'

'Good. I wouldn't want the other kids to tease him at school.'

Samantha could see that he wanted to touch the baby, hold it even, and in a way she wanted that to. Part of her wanted Tony as far away from the baby as possible but the other half wanted it to be him, rather than Stuart, who was bringing the baby home. In the drug-induced daze at the hospital she had even called out his name.

Tony brushed the baby's cheek with the middle of his finger. 'Look after him, won't you.' It was more of a demand than a question.

'So let us see him then,' said Mrs Haylett, all in a flap. She scooped the baby out of Sam's arms, clasping the bundle tight against her own chest. She glanced coldly at Tony. 'I'd better get him inside. In private.' And she turned and scurried back up the path.

Sandy hugged his daughter extra tight. 'Come on, love, you must be knackered.'

Stuart got to the gate, laden down with bags. He jerked his head to acknowledge Tony, who opened the gate for him with an exaggerated welcoming bow.

As Stuart struggled past, Tony leaned in. 'Well, he's an ugly little bastard, isn't he?' he hissed in Stuart's ear.

'Don't you dare say that.'

'Should have got rid of it when I told you to.' When Stuart had announced that Sam was pregnant, Tony tried to persuade Stuart it would be better to have an abortion. 'You don't know who that slag has been with,' he said.

'Fuck off,' said Stuart.

'There's always one runt in the pack.'

'Shut up. Fucking shut up.' Stuart was angry and it looked

as if he was about to headbutt Tony when Tony slapped him on the back and said, 'Sorry, mate. I was only joking. I'm just winding you up. Maybe I went a bit too far.'

'That's your problem; you always go too far. You never know when to stop.'

'Come on, mate. I didn't mean it. I'm glad they're both ok. I heard it wasn't easy.'

'It was dreadful. They thought the baby was going to die.'

'He's ok though, right? You got through it.'

'We'll have to wait and see. They want to do some tests.'

Tony looked genuinely concerned. He asked if Stuart would be going to the pub to celebrate the baby's birth, but Stuart looked exhausted and just shook his head. Then he started up the path to the house.

'I'll send Esther round,' shouted Tony after him. 'Who knows, it might get her broody again.'

Inside the house, Sam was with her parents. Her mum was dabbing her eyes with a cloth. Sandy was holding the baby.

'He's perfect, love.'

'He's not, Dad. You know he's not. Oh, don't cry, Mum. It just makes things worse. There were complications, that's all. It does not mean he's going to be damaged. We'll have to wait and see what the tests say.'

She looked at her dad holding the baby and for some reason felt sorry for him. Her mother just aggravated her.

'I don't want that Tony Fletcher hanging round here,' said Sandy. 'You've got Stuart now. He'll be a good father no matter what happens.'

Stuart stood in the hallway listening to them talking about him. The elation he had felt in the hospital was wearing off, leaving just exhaustion. He was determined to be a good father, just as Mr Haylett had said. He remembered the long two days that Sam had been in labour. How he had been constantly at her side, squeezing her hand and moping her brow, getting anything she wanted. And he had loved it. For perhaps the first time he had been truly needed and somehow the more difficult and complicated things became the closer he felt to Sam.

But then Tony had upset him with his stupid remarks, and he had thought of James and how caring for his brother was destroying him, turning him into an alcoholic. What if the baby was damaged? What if his brain wouldn't work? How would he and Sam cope then? Did he love her enough for them to survive something like that?

Perhaps he would have said yes a week ago, but a lot had happened since then. Becky had come back and opened up the possibilities of life outside Homerton and memories of that dreadful night five years ago. Then there was someone killing of the local cats. Suddenly everything was in turmoil.

Jason came down the stairs and grabbed Stuart's arm. 'I know about you and that Becky Sullivan,' he spat. 'Everyone says she's trouble.'

'You don't know anything,' said Stuart, pulling his arm free.

'Oh yeh, then what were you doing with her on Saturday night. People saw you so don't deny it. Are you going to tell Sam or shall I?'

'You wouldn't want to do that. Not now, not when she has just had a baby.'

'Then I'll just have to make you pay instead,' said Jason. He glared at Stuart. 'I could strangle your neck like those cats, that's what I could do.'

*

Esther was sitting in Becky's kitchen eating toast when her phone pinged with a new text. Excitedly, she told Becky that

Stuart and Samantha had finally come out of hospital with the baby. Then she went through the whole backstory of Stuart and Samantha's relationship.

'The rumour is the baby is not even Stuart's. Sam is not what you would call restrained when it comes to relationships. She has put herself around a bit. The father could be half a dozen men in the town.'

Becky told her Stuart had stayed the Saturday night and had been there when Samantha went into labour. It was typical of Becky to trump her own story. Esther asked whether she found Stuart attractive. 'It's not about that,' said Becky. 'He was around and sometimes that is enough.'

She changed the subject. 'What about you and Tony?' she asked. 'You've been together for a few years now. Any baby on the horizon?'

Esther lowered her head, twisting her hands in her lap.

'I'm sorry. It is none of my business. I shouldn't have asked.'

'No. It's ok. I don't want to think about children again, not yet, not after the miscarriage. And not with Tony. He's not really the dad sort is he? You know what he's like.'

Esther perked up, as if she had donned a new mask. She told Becky there was a wedding on Saturday – somebody they had been to school with – and pleaded with her to come along.

Becky said she wasn't sure. There had been a lot of interest in the cottage, and she was hoping to agree a sale by the end of the week. 'Then I can finally get away from this town with all its crap memories,' she said. She could see the hurt on Esther's face. 'Oh, fuck it. Of course, I'll come. We could both do with a party.'

*

'Oh, it's you.'

It was half-past-eleven and the clouds had cleared to leave

the black pin-pricked sky. It was freezing cold. Tony steadied himself against the door frame.

'You're drunk,' said Sandra Palmer. 'It's late.'

'I had to see you,' slurred Tony. 'I need some company.' He lurched forward to kiss her, but she stepped back, and he stumbled before pulling himself upright.

Sandra looked left and right along the street. 'You had better come in. I'm freezing with this door open. But be quiet, the kids are in bed.' She stood aside and Tony entered. 'I hope you are not going to waste my time,' she said, closing the door and ushering him into the sitting room.

14

The wedding was in St Mary's Church at two in the afternoon. Stephanie, who worked at a fitness centre in Acle, was marrying farmer's son Brendon. Half the town was invited. Guests milled round outside the church in the bright sunshine, the women fanning themselves beneath flowery hats, the men running fingers around the collars of stiff buttoned-up shirts and dabbing their foreheads with handkerchiefs. They moaned about the heat just as they had moaned about the rain the day before.

'Can't you wait?' huffed Esther.

'What?'

'Smoking. Couldn't you wait until after the service? Nobody else is smoking.' Sometimes everything Tony did aggravated her. Often, particularly at events like this, she was ashamed of him. His tie was loosely knotted and skewed, and she was tempted to lean forward and tighten it up but stopped herself. Tony blew a plume of smoke into her face.

'Another sucker getting hitched. He must need an extra pair of hands on the farm. I don't know who any of these people are.'

Brendon's father started shepherding the guests inside. Tony flicked his cigarette on to the path and crushed it with his foot.

Inside, one of the ushers directed them to the bride's side and Stephanie's mum thanked Esther for coming, saying it was good that some of Stephanie's old school friends were there.

The organist played Abba tunes as the guests shuffled along the pews.

'I can't believe you wore those,' said Esther, nodding towards Tony's cowboy boots.

Tony sighed. 'Pity James couldn't come.' He looked around for somebody other than Esther to talk to. Sandy Haylett and his wife were sitting on the row in front. Tony tapped Sandy on the shoulder.

'Your Sam's not coming then?'

Sandy did not turn around. 'Her and Stuart are at home with the baby.'

Jason glared at Tony. 'Probably best,' said Tony sitting back in the pew. He could sense Mr Haylett stiffen.

'Don't you start that with me, boy. They've got nothing to hide.'

For a second it looked as if Sandy might turn around and give Tony a mouthful, but Mrs Haylett patted his hand and muttered, 'Don't let him wind you up. Let's not ruin Steph's day.'

Esther was watching the church door. The sun was shining through the high window, and it illuminated her face like a renaissance Madonna. The other guests were seated when Becky came dashing in. Everybody in the church turned and there was whispering and tutting in the pews. The vicar gave a silencing cough. Becky found Esther and she mouthed the word "sorry" before moving to sit next to her.

'What's she doing here?' muttered Tony.

Then the organist started the wedding march and all the faces turned towards the front of the church. At the sound of the door opening, Brendon turned at the altar to smile at his future bride as she came down the aisle. The guests turned as well.

'She looks as if she's been crying,' said Becky giving Esther a nudge.

'Til death do us part…' Esther mumbled. 'Poor cow.'

*

'That really is a beautiful dress,' said Becky. Esther blushed. They were standing in the shade of the west tower whilst everyone had their picture taken with the bride and groom.

'I haven't been to a wedding in ages,' said Becky. 'But weddings are so much better than funerals.' She looked over at Tony who was walking around in circles, talking loudly into his phone and scuffing his feet on the ground.

'You should have stayed round here. There's one a week in summer. It's what passes for a social life in this place.' *Weddings and funerals*, thought Esther, *is that how my life is going to be measured?*

'I suppose Stuart and Sam will be next. Now they've got the baby.'

'Doubt it,' said Esther. 'You know Stuart. He's hardly the marrying kind. Besides, I'm not sure the Haylett's want *him* for a son-in-law.' She tipped her head on to her shoulder and pulled a mock questioning face. 'But what about you? You scrub up OK! Found anyone special yet?'

Becky laughed. 'Let's just say my relationships tend to get complicated.'

Just then, Stephanie came over and grabbed Esther's hand, dragging her for a group photo of all her friends. She smiled weakly at Becky as if to make the point she was not a friend and had not been invited.

'Go on,' said Becky. 'I'll cadge a fag off Tony.'

Becky found Tony round the back of the church, skulking between two of the buttresses. There was something starved and ghoulish about Tony as he stood there in the shadows.

Tony fished a packet of cigarettes from his pocket and offered one to Becky. She took the cigarette, and he lit it for her, cupping the lighter in his hand and bringing it up close to her face so that it burnt with a yellow glow. Becky tossed her head back as she inhaled deeply then blew a stream of smoke high into the air. Tony watched her and she was aware of his gaze. His face was close to hers, so close that if he had leaned forward he could have kissed her.

'Do you remember how we used to smoke behind the youth club?' asked Becky.

'We used to do more than smoke.'

She remembered and was transported back. It felt intimate, the two of them standing there, hiding away from the others, sharing a cigarette.

'Why did you come back, Becks? We'd almost forgotten you. And here you are messing it all up again.'

'I had to sell the cottage.'

Tony shook his head. 'It's more than that. You could have dealt with the estate agents from London.'

'Perhaps I needed a holiday. To get away. Things were a bit sticky in London.' Becky dropped her cigarette and stubbed it out.

'Yeh I can imagine. You seem to cause trouble wherever you go,' said Tony without meanness.

'I don't suppose you've exactly been a good boy,' said Becky. 'Though I never thought you would stick around here.'

'There are worse places,' said Tony, feeling a little hurt. 'Are you going to stay long?'

Becky shrugged. 'Once I've sold the house, I guess I'll be off.'

'You'll be worth a bit – what with the cottage. Then you'll abandon us again. Just like you did years ago.'

'You know it wasn't like that. My father made me go. Everyone thought it was for the best at the time. You know what it was like.'

Tony looked over at the graveyard. Two figures were crouched at one of the graves, laying flowers. It was James and Nick. 'Look at that sad fuck,' said Tony. 'He always was a sad fuck. He might as well be in the grave himself, having to look after that Nick day and night. No wonder he's a fucking alcoholic.'

*

The reception was held in the old stables at Cranham Manor. Guests were mingling before being called into the dining room for the meal. Waiters and waitresses meandered through the crowd dispensing drinks. It was nearly five in the afternoon.

'We'll have two of those,' said Esther, grabbing the glasses from a passing tray. She was standing with Becky, and they had been drinking for the past hour and a half. 'Bet you miss all this, don't you?' Esther said sarcastically.

'A bit.'

'But not enough to come back. I still don't know why you are here, Becky.'

'It was time to lay the ghosts to rest, to come to terms with what happened. I'm sick of fucking things up.'

'I don't understand.'

Becky leaned in drunkenly and whispered. 'Can I tell you a secret?' Esther nodded. 'The cottage. I'm going to give half the money to his wife. Pay her back, you know, for what we did. It's the only way I can get over it.'

'Yeh, I believe you.' Esther smiled. 'Come on, don't be an arse. That's just the drink talking.'

'It's not, it's not. I'm telling you the truth. For once I am going to do something good.'

Becky felt strangely intoxicated. It was hot in the room, and she had not eaten all day. But usually the drink numbed her rather than made her happy. Now she was tingling and excitable. 'Your Tony hasn't changed. Do you remember when he used to hang around the school trying to look cool. We all fancied him rotten.'

Becky was talking fast. The words fizzing in her mouth like the bubbles in her glass. She did not notice that Esther was not smiling.

'Who would have thought you two would end up together. The bad boy and Little Miss Prim?'

Esther drank her wine in one go and was looking around for another. Tony had gone off to do some business after the church service and Esther was glad he was not around. She wished Becky would stop talking about him.

'We all looked like good girls next to you,' said Esther. She thought about Becky and Stuart and how she had fallen into bed with someone within days of returning. She caught the attention of a waitress and beckoned her over.

'You are wasting your time if you think you can tame him, Est. Tony will always be a bad boy. That's what makes him so exciting. You might as well just enjoy him for what he is.'

Stuart, James and Tony turned up together just after six. It was clear they had been drinking and their loud voices and demands for beer drew scornful looks from some of the guests. Stuart headed straight for the buffet table and started hoovering up what was left of the food, stuffing drooping canapes and dry sandwiches into his face.

Becky told James that she had seen him earlier in the graveyard with Nick. 'That was sweet of you,' she said.

The mention of Nick's name made James anxious. 'Was

it? Nick insists we go but it only upsets him. He would be better off not being reminded that his mum is dead.' He looked exhausted. He made it clear to Becky that he wanted to forget about Nick for a few hours and he pulled her away to get a drink from the bar.

Esther was very drunk; drunk in an intense way, as if the alcohol was burning away inside her. She had trouble standing upright and was propped against the edge of the table with her arms. Tony sneered at her in disgust. He grabbed her left arm and pushed his face into her left ear.

'Look at you. You should be ashamed of yourself. Everyone is looking at you.'

'I'm just a bit tipsy, that's all. I'm having a bit of fun. You're always telling me to lighten up and have some fun.'

'You're a disgrace.'

Tony jerked his head away from her, but his hand gripped her arm tighter. He wanted to squeeze it dry, to grip it so hard her bones would snap.

'Tony, you are hurting me. Let go of my fucking arm.'

She felt the vice loosen and his hand fall away. Tony was scanning the room. He stopped when he saw Becky at the bar. Stuart had joined her and James.

'She was talking about you earlier,' said Esther over his shoulder.

Tony turned. 'What did she say?'

'Oh, only what a bad boy you were. How there is no point in trying to tame you. Maybe you need a bad girl.' She puckered her lips and took his hand and pulled it towards her body, but Tony snatched it back.

Tony's lips were twisted with contempt. There was anger in his eyes. 'You stupid ugly cow.'

He looked back over at Becky.

'You're wasting your time there,' Esther slurred. 'She's

already fucked Stuart. Last Saturday after the pub. He stayed the night. She told me all about it. All the fucking details.'

Tony turned again. Across Esther's mouth was a stupid drunken grin. Tony's face turned ashen white. It was as if his features were being screwed into his head; his nose seemed to shrink into his cheeks; his eyes became black holes. He raised his arm.

For a moment Esther thought he was going to hit her, and she recoiled, but he brought his fist down with a thump into his own left hand.

Stuart and Becky were joking about babies. James stood silently beside them, watching Becky's mouth as she joked along, the sound of her laughter like a bird escaping from a cage.

Stuart's relief to be away from Sam and back with his old friends was palpable. He was drinking to sustain the mood, to ride the good times, to drag out each minute.

'The problem's not Sam and the baby.' He nodded to the other side of the room where the Haylett's were sitting. 'It's them. They can't stand me, and they make it obvious.'

'I am sure that's not true,' said Becky. 'Sandy is OK. He was my dad's mate.'

'That's part of the problem. He knows too much about what happened.'

Out of nowhere and almost to himself, James said they had found another cat that morning up on the staithes, bringing down the mood and attracting a glare from Stuart. It was clear it was something that troubled James. He looked twitchy.

'I reckon it's that Jason,' said Stuart. 'He's a nutter. He's always skulking around. He's weird. You ought to see the way he looks at you. You don't want to meet him late at night, I can tell you. He'd bite your neck if it was a full moon.'

Stuart leaned into the bar, holding up a tenner to try and get the barmaids attention. Becky turned to James. He was sweating. 'I might go back soon,' he said. 'And check on Nick. Just to make sure. Everyone thinks he can cope but he can't, not always.'

Tony came thundering over to the bar. He was bristling with anger. He shoved against Stuart's back, making him spill his drink.

'Hey, watch it,' said Stuart, turning. James put his hand on Stuart's arm to stop him reacting.

'So, you've dumped Sam and the baby already,' said Tony. 'You never were reliable.'

'What's got on your nerves?'

'You have, you little shit.' Tony grabbed Stuart by the lapels and pulled his face forward, spraying him with spit. 'Couldn't keep your dick to yourself, could you?' He glanced over at Becky.

'I don't know what you mean.'

James tried to put his arm between them, but Tony brushed him aside. James tugged at Stuart's elbow to pull him away.

'You and her,' said Tony. James gave Becky a questioning look. 'You couldn't fucking wait, could you? Even though Sam was expecting a baby, you had to jump into bed with another woman.'

Stuart stepped back, shaking off Tony's grip. As he did so, he knocked his drink and it splashed on Tony. 'Oh, grow up. She's not your property.'

'I am nobody's property,' said Becky trying to make light of it. Tony went to grab her, but she turned to avoid him.

'Come on. Cool it, you two.' James put his arm round Stuart's shoulder and began to steer him away from the bar.

'Fucking psychopath,' muttered Stuart.

Tony's hand came down on his shoulder and he spun him around. Suddenly his fist was flying into Stuart's face. There was a crack as his knuckles smashed into Stuart's nose. Stuart flew back against a table, sending glasses into the air before shattering on the floor. James stumbled against the bar. Becky screamed for them to stop and from across the room Esther shouted Tony's name.

Stuart struggled up. Blood was pouring from his nose and mouth. He wiped the back of his hand across his face. Stuart lurched at Tony. Tony blocked his punch with his left arm. He drove his right fist into Stuart's gut, winding him and sending him reeling backwards.

Space cleared around them like ripples across a pond. The bride was sobbing, and her father was angrily shouting at them to stop. The groom looked as if he had suddenly realised his marriage was doomed.

Sandy ran over from the other side of the hall, scattering chairs as he stormed towards them. He yanked Stuart upright and dragged him away. James stood in front of Tony to stop him going after them saying, 'Enough, Tony, enough.' A siren sounded outside. 'Get out of here, quick.'

Tony pulled himself together, found the exit and scarpered towards it. As he was going out the door, someone pushed past him in a fluster. 'There's a fire,' he shouted to everyone in the hall. 'At the garage. The place is full of smoke.'

He saw James over by the bar. 'James, come on. The fire brigade is on its way.' James ran after him and several of the guests followed them outside. Sandy Haylett took Stuart away. Becky went over to Esther, who was bent forward with her head in her hands. She was crying.

'Things are fucked up,' she sobbed. Becky gently stroked the top of Esther's hair. Esther raised her face. It was wet with tears.

Becky bent down and kissed Esther on the forehead. She took her hands and helped her up saying, 'Come on, Est, James needs us.'

15

It was half-past-ten on the Sunday morning when Esther returned from visiting James and Nick. The damage to the garage was not as bad as expected. One wall of the kitchen was black with smoke and the kitchen window was charred. The cooker was a wreck. But given the amount of smoke billowing out of the place the previous night, the impact of the fire had been minimal.

Tony was still in bed. Esther inched open the door to the bedroom and stood looking at him curled on top of the duvet. If she had ever needed confirmation of his desire for Becky, last night had provided it. It was clear he could not abide the thought of her being with another man. She regretted telling him about Becky and Stuart, but it was too late now. Looking at him lying there, she could only feel loathing – not just against him but also with herself for having been such a fool to believe he ever truly loved her.

Tony stirred. His eyes unglued then closed again. He stretched and turned over on to his back. He raised his arms behind his head then crossed them into a pillow. Suddenly he was alert. He squinted at Esther standing on the other side of the room.

'What are you standing there like that for?' He noticed her jacket. 'Where have you been?'

'I went to see James. They are both OK if you are interested. Nick burnt his arm a bit, that's all.'

Tony laughed. 'Do you think I care about that fat idiot. It would be better for everyone if he had gone up in flames. He's a waste of space. He should have been put down at birth.'

'Don't be like that, Tony. James is our friend, and it has really shaken him up. His brother is all he has got left.'

'He's not my friend.' Tony sniffed. 'He's spineless.'

'You will never let it go, will you? Something that happened years ago and still you won't forgive him for running out. When are we ever going to put that night behind us?'

'He's a coward. He deserves to be stuck with that idiot.'

Tony had gone too far, and he knew it. He rolled on to his side and propped his head up on his hand. Esther went over to the wardrobe and Tony watched her as she crossed the room. He told her that she was looking pretty and that he liked it when she stood up for others.

'Come over here.'

She turned and went and sat on the end of the bed. The shoulder of her dress had slipped a little and Tony looked at where her hair tumbled over the nape of her neck. Sometimes he forgot how attractive she was. He sat up and pulled her towards him.

'Come on, why don't you come back to bed.'

She fell against his legs then sat back up. 'I've got to go to work. We open at eleven.'

'That's another hour,' said Tony. 'Come on, I'm in the mood.'

Esther struggled free of his grip and stood up. She smoothed down her dress and tossed back her hair before fixing it into a ponytail with a band.

'You're never up for it these days,' said Tony.

'Perhaps I don't feel wanted,' said Esther. 'I can't turn it on and off like you can. Perhaps if you didn't make me feel second best…'

'Here we go. What the hell does that mean?'

Esther looked at him as if he was her enemy. 'Last night. You and Stuart fighting over Becky like that. Like schoolboys. How do you think it makes me feel? It makes me feel like shit. You would never fight for me like that. It's clear you still fancy her. I wish to God she hadn't come back.'

'Oh, don't be so pathetic. You were in a right state last night. You have no idea what happened. You were so fucking drunk I'm surprised you can remember anything.'

Esther lunged at Tony with her fist, but he caught her wrist and twisted it sharply, causing her to yelp. He pushed her backwards and she stumbled against the edge of the bed. She regained her balance and lurched at him again this time landing a slap across his face. She stepped back in shock, but he just snorted. 'What did you do that for? Get out of my sight.'

Esther turned and left the bedroom with tears trickling down her face.

*

'He's asleep,' said James gently, closing the bedroom door. Relief washed across his face. He asked Becky if she wanted another drink. She drank down the remains of her wine and nodded.

'You not having one?' she asked.

'Not tonight,' said James. 'I am so worried about Nick. I need a clear head right now.' He rubbed his hands and Becky could see the anxiety returning. He looked as if he had not slept for days, and black shadows drooped under his eyes. His hair was a mess, and he was dressed in an old tee shirt and shorts.

'He could have killed himself. I'm not sure I can leave him alone anymore.'

He took Becky's glass as he went past and filled it from the bottle that was on the kitchen counter. 'I haven't got much in, I'm afraid. Foodwise. I just haven't had time to get to the shops.'

Becky told him not to worry. She asked him what he was going to do about Nick.

James looked bemused. 'What do you mean?'

'Well, in the long-term. You can't look after him full time and run the garage. It will burn you out. You need help.'

'Are you saying I can't cope?'

'No, it's just…'

'I'm not putting him in a home if that's what you mean. I am not going to abandon him. Not like you abandoned your dad.' He was agitated and almost spitting with anger.

Becky was shocked. 'I didn't abandon my dad. He sent me away until things blew over. He said it was best I was not around.'

'You didn't rush back though, did you? He ended up a lonely, broken man. Drinking himself into a stupor every night. He talked about you all the time.'

'Don't be so horrible,' said Becky tearfully. 'It wasn't like that. I couldn't come back. Don't you think I would have helped him if I could, but I couldn't face it, not then. It would have destroyed me.'

'You didn't even come back for his funeral.'

'I wasn't ready.'

'But you are now?'

Becky nodded. She told James how the sale of the cottage provided a chance to make amends by giving a share from the sale to Mrs Palmer.

'I could help you out as well. If you need money for Nick or the garage.'

Just then a siren went past outside. James jumped. 'I don't want your bloody money, Becky,' he said.

It was drizzling when Becky left, and a swirling fog had come in from the sea and settled on the town. Becky felt she had said everything she had to say to James and now it was time to leave Homerton. All she had to do was finalise the sale of the cottage, give some money to Sandra Palmer and she would be gone. She was walking across the green when she heard an urgent voice calling her name. Tony emerged from the fog, running towards her. He reached out and grabbed her arms.

'Thank God I found you. I went to the cottage but you weren't there. Something terrible has happened.' He was short of breath and his eyes were bulging. He looked like a person who had woken with a start from a nightmare.

'What is it, Tony?'

'It's Esther. She's tried to kill herself.' He was shaking. Becky put her arm around him.

'When? How?'

'I don't know. I came back an hour ago and she was lying in the bath. I tried to stop the blood. I phoned the ambulance straight away. Oh, what am I going to do? It was my fault, Becky. I should have been there for her.'

He was limp and Becky was holding him up. Their faces were wet with the drizzle and tears. 'Why didn't you go with her, Tony? In the ambulance? You should be with her.'

16

'Becky, come and join us.' Stuart stood up and beckoned her over. It was Monday lunchtime in the Fisherman's Return and Stuart was at a table with Sam and Mr and Mrs Haylett. Becky paid for her glass of wine and went to join them. There was an obvious coldness towards her from everyone but Stuart, due no doubt to the fight a couple of nights before at the wedding reception and what had caused it. Sam was huddled next to Stuart on one of the banquettes, holding his hand as if she was scared to let go.

'Sam and I have set a date for the wedding, so we are out to celebrate.' He smiled like someone who has not got the punchline of a joke. Mr and Mrs Haylett looked as if a death had been announced.

'So when is it then?' asked Becky sitting down.

'The 15th of September,' said Sam. 'The sooner the better really, now little Tyson is here.' She glanced at one end of the table where the baby was asleep in its pram. 'We said why wait any longer, didn't we, Stu? There's no point really. Specially since Dad has managed to get a little flat for us. I can't wait to be Mrs Bushell.' She snuggled into Stuart.

'Jason not toasting the good news?' asked Becky.

This was clearly a sensitive issue with Mr Haylett. 'He's working. Which is where I should be.'

'He was home late last night,' Stuart interjected. 'I don't think he could face the pub this morning.'

'You can talk, boy,' said Sandy Haylett sharply. 'You weren't in much of a state on Saturday night yourself. At least he don't go getting into fights.' He cut a glance over to Becky as if to say, "I know who is to blame".

'I said it was nothing,' said Stuart. 'It was just a misunderstanding with Tony. Nothing serious.' He looked down lovingly at Sam. 'Let's not ruin the celebration.'

Sam seemed uneasy. 'I don't want to talk about Tony, Dad. Not today. He's bad news, always has been.' She leaned over and peered into the pram. 'Well, I don't want him leading you astray, Stuart, that's all. You're a dad now and you will soon be my husband. You can't go getting into trouble because of him.'

Mrs Haylett said she felt a migraine coming on and Mr Haylett said he would take her home. Sam said she would go with them as Tyson would need his feed. Mr Haylett prodded Stuart to come as well but he didn't get the message, saying he would stay and finish his pint.

'Sorry about that,' said Stuart when they had left.

'You poor sod,' said Becky. 'Are you sure you know what you are doing – with Sam, I mean. You don't have to throw your life away just because of the baby.'

'It's not like that. I really love her. I am sorry about last Saturday. I don't know what came over me. I was drunk.'

'Thanks a lot,' snorted Becky. 'You sure know how to make a girl feel wanted.'

'It's not like that. Of course not.' Stuart hesitated. 'You've really stirred things up, coming back after all these years. It might be some form of closure for you but for the rest of us – well, it's like somebody's gone and thrown a great big fucking brick in the middle of the pond. Tony said you coming back would be trouble…'

'Did he now?'

'Sorry, but he was right. Best let sleeping dogs lie.'

Becky leaned across and touched Stuart's hand. 'That's the last thing you should do,' she said.

'The problem is, Tony still fancies you. You know that. He has been in love with you since school. Poor Esther, she was always going to be second choice. If you really want to help her now, you should leave.'

*

'Is that it?' asked Becky. She handed him back the agreement and put the pen down on the table.

'Yes. All done. You can leave the rest to me.'

The solicitor had come over from Thorpe Bay and was sitting in the front room of the cottage. Sunlight was streaming in from the front window and had landed on his bald head. He wiped it with his handkerchief.

'All that is left is to dot the i's and cross the t's. It should take a couple of days but there is no need for you to hang around. They don't want to move in until next month. I'll let you know when the contracts are exchanged then bingo.'

He slipped the agreement into his folder. 'You are two hundred grand richer.'

He looked like a midwife who had successfully delivered another baby. He made no attempt to leave. He chuckled to himself. Becky asked if he wanted a drink to celebrate and he pretended to be surprised at the offer.

Ten minutes later he was standing at the window with a glass of wine in his hand. 'It's a lovely little town this,' he said, turning. 'Of course, there are no jobs round here. I guess that is why you are moving out?'

'I haven't lived here for years. It is my dad's house.'

'Oh well. Perhaps for the best then.'

Becky saw him out and returned to the room, which seemed suddenly empty. She took a gulp of her wine. This is what she wanted. It was a big step in putting the place behind her. Now there was nothing left in Homerton. The cottage where she had grown up would now be somebody else's home and other children would become adults there. The last ties with her father had been severed. At last she would be free to get on with her life.

*

'Get away from here. You are not welcome.'

'I just wanted…'

'Wanted what? To be forgiven? I don't care what you've got to say. I don't know how you can show your face around here again,' said Sandra Palmer. She was bent down and shouting through the letterbox which she had propped open with her fingers. She had opened the door not knowing it was Becky and had immediately tried to shut it again.

Becky had managed to get her arm inside, saying, 'I've got to talk to you.' But Sandra had shoved it out and had closed the door.

Becky was now standing on the porch repeatedly pressing the doorbell. From the living room, the boys kept shouting, 'There's someone at the door.'

'You can press that all you like but you're not coming in here. You've done enough damage to our lives. Why don't you just leave us alone. You should never have come back here.' Her voice cracked and she gave a little sob. She called back into the house, 'Fucking shut up and watch the telly.'

Becky bent down so that she was balanced on the balls of her feet, steadying herself against the door. She peered in at the letterbox.

'It's important,' said Becky. 'I know I am to blame, and I want to apologise. To make amends. I've got some money for you. From the sale of the house. I know it can never be enough, but if you let me in… I really do want to put things right.' Becky stood up. It was hot and she took off her jacket and folded it over her arm. Sweat dampened the curls of her hair on her neck. She was about to leave when she heard the door open.

'You'd better come in then,' said Sandra, stepping aside.

She sent the boys up to their room. She didn't offer Becky a drink. The room was a tip, with toys and school stuff scattered across the floor and a pile of washing in one corner. The wallpaper was torn in places and there was a rip across the back of the sofa.

At first they sat in stiff silence, then Sandra asked, 'What exactly happened on the night my Alistair died? I need to know.' She leaned forward. Her features were tense. 'Don't dare lie to me. I want the truth.'

And Becky told her everything. How she had seduced her husband and then used it by threatening to go to the police if he did not pay up. How he had a heart attack and there was nothing they could do to help him.

Becky found it easy to talk. The words came crashing out. It was if the dam behind which her painful memories had been held was suddenly broken and the memories came tumbling out. Her hands could not stay still. She needed a cigarette.

Sandra listened to it all in a daze. Becky had told her nothing new, nothing that she had not already imagined a thousand times. She sat looking at Becky as though she was looking through her. She was rigid. She turned away as if she could no longer bear to look at her.

'I was just a child,' said Becky. 'We didn't know what we were doing. How did we know he was going to have a heart attack? I know we should have owned up. I have regretted that ever since. But I want you to have this.' She took a cheque from the pocket of her jacket that was folded on her lap. It was for a hundred grand. She handed the cheque to Sandra and stood up to leave. 'I know it can never be enough,' she said.

Ten minutes after Becky left, Tony appeared at the back door and let himself into the kitchen.

'What did she want?' he asked.

'To confess,' said Sandra.

'I told you she was to blame. Her and Esther. The rest of us were just hangers-on. We did what she told us. Becky was the one who led everything. She was the one who was threatening him, and Esther egged her on. That's why they a both so eaten up with it.'

He leaned forward to kiss her, but she stepped back. 'How is Esther? She is still in hospital, isn't she?'

'I told you, she only did it to stop me leaving her. She knew I was going to end it with her.'

'But you didn't. You never do.'

'I couldn't – and I can't, not now. Not after she has tried to top herself. I've got to give it a bit of time.'

*

The hospital was in Great Yarmouth and Becky had to get two buses to get there. She sat on the top deck and looked out at the countryside. The yellow fields and clumps of trees, the neat flint cottages and lonely churches were embedded in her visual memory. She had seen the same picture every day from the window of the school bus. But she had forgotten how breathtaking the landscape could be on a sunny day when it was spread out before you for miles and the only things to break the stillness were the occasional crow taking flight or the sleepy swish of a cow's tail.

Esther was at the end of the ward. Her arms were resting on the top of the bedcovers with bandages around her wrists. She had her headphones in and did not notice Becky's arrival until she was standing next to the bed. Becky bent down and kissed Esther on the cheek. Esther took off her headphones. For a few minutes they joked about the other patients in the ward and Esther described a particularly dishy doctor who had been on the morning round. Becky apologised for not bringing anything, joking that they had confiscated the bottle of gin at the reception. She looked at the bandages and asked, 'Why did you do it, Est?'

'I don't know. It suddenly seemed like the only thing left I could do. I wasn't thinking straight. All I wanted was to get out.'

Becky said she was glad that Tony had come back in time. Esther shook her head. 'Why do you always defend him, Becks? Even after all these years? You coming back is part of the reason why I am lying here. He had almost gotten over you. Then you came back, and it was clear Tony still loved you.'

'I won't be around much longer,' said Becky and she realised how bad that sounded. Like she had come back and messed up their lives again and was now running away once more. Now this had happened. One of the people she had wanted to protect was lying in hospital with slashed wrists and instead of coming to terms with past events she had just stirred them up again.

'Tony and me, we are over, Becks. I am leaving him as soon as I get out of here. I realise I don't love him anymore and I sure as hell know he doesn't love me.' She shot a glance at Becky but not in a nasty way. 'We are finished,' said Esther and she turned away. 'It was always you he loved.'

Just when Becky was getting ready to leave Homerton for good, the situation had changed. Becky knew she had to leave;

she had come back to end things not to start them up again. She had to remain focused. If she dithered now, she would regret it for the rest of her life. Tony was no good, she knew that. Yet she hesitated before saying, 'I am surprised you stayed with him for so long. He's an absolute pig and you deserve better.' But her words did not ring true.

17

Becky was surprised to hear Tony's voice on the other end of the line. She had forgotten how startling the ringing of a phone in an empty house could be. It was nearly one in the afternoon, and she was still not fully awake.

'She refuses to see me,' Tony whined. 'I went all the way to the hospital, and she told the bleeding nurse to keep me away. She's not thinking straight. Of course, I blame myself for what has happened. I should have seen the signs. She has been like a fucking emotional yo-yo for months. Then you turned up…'

'Don't try and blame this on me,' said Becky.

'I'm not,' said Tony. 'Of course, I'm not. It's just that I should have known. She was pretty fragile anyway. I should have been on guard.'

He sounded full of remorse, his voice strained with worry and regret. Becky felt like a Samaritan. 'What am I going to do?' wailed Tony. 'It is definitely over between us. We were making each other so unhappy. Our marriage was like a fridge. We were both so lonely.'

Then he dropped a bombshell. He confessed that he was the father of Sam's baby, and that Sam knew but had begged him to keep it secret. Her dad would kick her out if he knew she had slept with Tony. He had tried to get her to have an abortion, but she was not having it and she had started seeing Stuart to cover the whole thing up.

The only person Tony had told was Becky and that was because he had always trusted her. Becky wished he had not.

'It's eating me up,' Tony said. 'Seeing Sam and the baby around town, knowing it is mine and that Stuart is being duped. The thought of my baby in the same house as that nutter Jason…'

'Poor Esther,' said Becky.

'She doesn't know a thing,' said Tony, as if that made it alright.

Tony started talking about how low he felt and how he had thought about ending things. He begged Becky to see him one last time and she agreed to meet him that evening for a walk along the beach.

*

As Becky reached the top of the path from the town up to the cliffs, she could see that Tony was already there even though it was still only a quarter to seven. He was standing smoking, kicking the dirt with his feet with his head bowed as if he was trying to sort out a difficult problem in his head.

Grey clouds hung in the evening sky; their frayed edges singed bright orange by the sun. It was still warm. Becky stopped. She needed to go over in her head again what it was she was going to say to Tony. She had decided that this was the last time she was going to see him. He had messed up her life. Part of her hated him. But she knew he could also be funny and when he spoke to you it felt as if his attention was on you alone. He was exciting because you never knew what he was going to do next. Becky stopped herself. He was getting in her head again, working his way into her thoughts. She must not let that happen. She had decided that she would go for a short walk with him along the beach. She would tell him to move on from Esther and that it was his fault Esther was leaving. She would wish him luck and then say goodbye. She would be back in the cottage before it was dark and leave the next day, putting Homerton behind her forever.

'I'm glad you came,' said Tony. 'I thought you might have second thoughts, after what happened to Esther. Well she's your friend isn't she and...'

'Come on, let's go down to the beach,' said Becky, 'before it gets too dark.'

They went down the slope to the beach. The tide was out, and the beach was almost empty. Seagulls swooped above them. They walked towards Dunton. They must have walked for over an hour and a half, but Becky did not notice the time. Tony asked her all about her life since she had left Homerton; he asked her about her mother and the loss of her father. He listened as she told him all about the life she led in London. He barely mentioned what he had done over the past five years, dismissing it as boring when she tried to ask about it.

Becky found it easy to talk to Tony. She found his interest in her flattering. As they walked, she became more relaxed and forgot about what had happened to Esther. By the time they got back to the slope, it was almost dark and it had grown cold. Becky shivered. 'Here take this,' said Tony. He took off his jacket and draped it on her shoulders. He put his arm around her and pulled her close to his side. She crossed her arms in front of her and let herself snuggle under his arm.

Tony eased her towards the boulders at the bottom of the slope and they sat together on them. He reached over and pulled a quart bottle of whisky from his jacket. He poured some into the cap and gave it to Becky, saying it would warm her up. For the next hour they sat and watched the sea turn dark as the blinking lights of the container ships floated out across the North Sea; the night sky sparkled above them.

'I always thought you would be the one to leave here first,' said Becky, suddenly smitten by the beauty of the beach at night. 'Remember how you used to tell us about all the things you were going to do with your life. You always had such big plans. What happened to you, Tony?'

She felt him pull her closer towards him. 'You know how it is. Things happen and before you know it, years have gone by. Stuff crowds around you and it becomes harder to go. People depend on you.'

Becky felt sorry for him. For the first time he seemed vulnerable. The whisky was warm in her stomach. 'Esther, you mean?'

'Yeh maybe. It was a mistake from the start, Becks, you must know that. She was always my second choice. After you left, it was the nearest thing to being with you.' His face was close to hers and Becky was tempted to inch forward and kiss him, but she pulled away and stood up, saying it was too cold to stay on the beach.

As soon as she stood up, Becky felt drunk. It was dark and cold on top of the cliffs and there was no one else around. Tony took Becky's hand.

'Let's go over there for some shelter,' he said, pulling her towards the fisherman's cabin. As they got there, Becky turned and their mouths locked together in a passionate kiss. Tony pushed her against the side of the hut, his hand against her crotch. Becky felt his other hand scoop behind her head and pull it towards his. He kissed her neck and ears. His mouth slid over her cheek and locked back on to her lips.

'Stop,' said Becky. She slipped from his embrace. 'This isn't right.' She shook herself down and straightened her shirt.

'Esther is still in hospital, for Christ's sake. And this place…
with it's horrible memories.'

Tony was not listening. He took her hand and kissed it.
He reached up and stroked her hair. His touch was gentle. He
leaned forward and kissed the soft side of her neck. 'Esther
and I are finished. You know that,' whispered Tony. 'You are
leaving tomorrow, and I will never see you again. This is our
last chance. I want you so badly, Becky. I have always loved
you.'

He nibbled her ear, and she felt a tingle of excitement run
through her body. Tony pressed against her, his hand cupping
her breast through her shirt. He felt her soften beneath his
touch and her legs buckle. Becky's mouth opened and her
breathing grew heavy.

'Come with me,' said Tony, as he guided her inside the hut,
showering her with kisses. Tony quickly lit some candles that
were standing on a table that ran along one side of the room.
He took the jacket from Becky's shoulders and lay it on the
floor. She pushed her body against Tony. He tugged her bra
aside and grabbed at her breasts, rolling her nipples between
his fingers. He slid his other hand down the back of her jeans,
lifting her from the floor as he seized her buttocks. He was
biting and kissing her neck. She covered his face in kisses in
return. She tossed her head back. The cabin swirled around
them.

'Stop,' demanded Becky. 'I can't do this.' He kissed her
as she spoke, silenced her. She tried to wriggle free, but Tony
was too strong and he did not stop. He pushed himself harder
against her, trying to force her down on to the floor. She
kicked out but the tightness of their embrace meant she had no
power. She tried to hit him with her fists, but he just pressed
closer against her. She bit his arm and his grip loosened for a
moment, enabling her to shake herself free. She stumbled over

Tony's feet and crashed against the table, knocking the candles on to the floor.

Tony grabbed her wrist to stop her escaping and pulled her back towards him. 'I'm not letting you go, not this time,' he shouted. He was too powerful for Becky. His nostrils were flared, and his eyes were full of determination. His other hand gripped Becky's right arm and he dragged her back into his chest. He used the full weight of his body to push her down on to the floor, kicking her legs from beneath her so she fell roughly on to the floor.

She grazed her hand as she tried to stop her fall, but Tony collapsed on top of her, pinning her to the ground. She tried to struggle out from underneath him, but it was no good. He was too heavy, and he rammed his shoulders into hers to stop her moving. He pushed his right leg between hers to lever them open. Becky tried to scream but Tony covered her mouth with his hand. She attempted to bite his fingers and rocked her head from side to side to get it free.

Tony was grunting. He tore at her shirt and then reached down with his right hand to rip her jeans open, but he could not get them undone.

It was growing hot. Some rags under the table had caught on fire from the candles and flames were flicking up along one side of the cabin. Becky could feel the heat burning her face. The floor turned hot. Black smoke started to fill the room and it became difficult to breath.

Tony was still trying to pull her jeans down. Becky slammed her fist down on his back, but her strength had deserted her, and her hand fell weakly to her side. Becky fainted.

Tony saw her eyes close and he felt her body become limp. It was as if he had suddenly woken from a nightmare.

'Becky. Becky,' he screamed. He shook her face to try and wake her up. He struggled to his feet. The smoke was choking him. He tried to pull her up, but he could not, and she fell back like a dead weight onto the floor.

The hut was now full of dense smoke and flames were filling the room. Tony was dizzy and confused from the smoke. He was coughing and spluttering. He picked up a bottle from the corner of the cabin and smashed it against the window, but it just ricocheted off. He picked up another and this time threw it with all his might. It hit the window and crashed through, shattering on the ground outside. He bent down again to try and drag Becky up.

There was a thump against the door of the hut, then another and another. Someone was shouting, 'I'm coming!' The door crashed to the floor, followed by James who fell into the hut. He grabbed Tony and yanked him outside retching from the smoke.

He saw Becky on the floor. By now the whole hut was on fire. James covered his mouth and bent down and dashed to where she was lying. He grabbed her arms and pulled her up. Then he turned her round and dragged her backwards by her arms from the hut. He pulled her across the grass until they were safely away from the cabin.

Tony was sitting with his head against his knees. 'What the fuck were you doing,' James shouted at Tony. 'You're a fucking lunatic. You could have both died. You will pay for this, Tony, I swear you will.'

Becky spluttered back to life and James took his jacket and covered her up. He gave her a sip of water. Becky looked over at Tony. His head was buried in his hands. She turned away. The side of her face was hot. She reached up to touch it, but James stopped her.

'Don't,' he said. 'Wait until the ambulance gets here. You've got a bad burn there. We'll need to get you to hospital.'

He took out his phone and called 999. By now, the hut

was ablaze and a couple of cars were coming up from the town.

James looked over at Tony. 'People are coming,' he said. 'You might not want to be around when they get here. You better make yourself scarce.' But Tony did not move.

Becky touched her face delicately with her fingers. The skin had been burnt off, exposing the raw cheek below. A burning sensation seared through her face. *This is my punishment*, she thought. *It is retribution for what I have done.*

18

The next morning, the sun rose and turned the sky purple, then pink and then a clear crystal blue. Becky emptied a few things from the drawer in the bedroom and, together with the couple of items from the top of the dresser, tipped them into a black bag. Then she called the taxi firm and booked a cab for half-past-six that evening.

Dr Matthewson snapped off his surgical gloves and dropped them in the medical-waste bin. He raised the blinds and sun streamed into the consulting room. The doctor had tight curly ebony hair, thick lips and fat cheeks. His eyes were trained never to meet directly those of his patients.

He sat down opposite Becky, leaned over and picked up her file from his desk. He opened the file and took a pen from his breast pocket. He made a few notes in the file. He sucked the top of the pen then he closed the file and returned it to his desk. He looked somewhere between the corner of Becky's mouth and the lobe of her right ear.

'Well, I am afraid it was a nasty little burn. Although I expect it might heal over in a week or so, there is a risk of permanent scarring. A mark on the side of your face that will look a bit different from the skin around it.' Becky watched his lips move as he spoke, but she was only half listening to what he had to say. 'We can explore the possibility of some repair surgery in a few months. When we know how the ground lies. A small graft maybe. We will see.'

Becky turned and looked at her face in the mirror. There was an area of her cheek about two inches in diameter where the skin had been burnt away, leaving a raw, red patch of flesh. The skin around it was flaking. *This is the face I deserve*, thought Becky. *I should carry this mark for the rest of my life as a sign of the dreadful things I have done.*

She turned back to the doctor and smiled. 'Thanks, Doctor, you've been a great help. As you say, let's wait and see what happens.'

She stood up and went to the door and Dr Matthewson watched her, thinking he would not see a patient with a sexier figure in a long time.

She went down to the ward where Esther was staying. Esther was sitting on the bed taking a few items from the bedside cabinet and putting them in her overnight bag.

'You leaving?'

'Yes, they've given me the all-clear. I'm not mad anymore.'

Esther stared at the scar on Becky's face. 'What happened?'

'There was a fire in the fisherman's hut.'

'I know,' said Esther. 'James came to see me earlier. He told me you were trapped. Oh, Becks it must have been awful. Will it scar?' asked Esther, looking at the mark and thinking, against her better judgement, how it was perhaps not a bad thing for Becky to know what it was like to be flawed.

'Maybe, they don't know yet.'

'Are you OK about that?' Becky nodded. 'I hear that Tony's in custody. It wasn't right what he did, Becks. He's a bastard. I don't know what you were thinking but I don't blame you. He's always manipulating people. They will throw the book at him. They've been wanting to get him on something for years.

I hope he rots in prison.' Esther zipped up her bag. She said she was going back to the flat in Homerton whilst Tony was not there to pack up her things. Her parents had given her some money to tide her over.

'I am leaving Homerton for good. I am sick of it and everything that has happened here. I should have left years ago like you did but I never had the guts. Now is my chance. One of my dad's friends has got a flat in Cambridge I can use, so I'll go there to start with. I just need to put everything behind me. There is nothing left for me in Homerton now. As for Tony, I never want to see him again. I need a fresh start. Perhaps I will go off and actually do something with my life.' Esther stood up. 'What about you?'

Becky said the sale of the cottage had gone through and that she had given half of the money to Mrs Palmer. 'I'm going as well. I am leaving this evening, back to London. Perhaps we can meet up if you ever come down there? I would like that, Est. Just you and me.'

They stood awkwardly for a moment, not knowing how to say goodbye. Neither of them knew what the other was feeling and for a moment they were strangers. Esther winced when she tried to lift her bag from the floor.

'Come here, you silly mare,' said Becky. 'Let's get a cab back to Homerton together. I can help you clear out your things.'

'Look at us two,' said Esther holding up her bandaged wrists and looking at Becky's scar. 'Both of us damaged by the same man.'

'Not anymore. I've been scared half my life, Esther, and I refuse to be scared anymore.'

*

In the police station at Hemsby, Sergeant Cleaver was questioning Tony. He had admitted the sexual assault on Becky as soon as the police arrived at the fire, and he had signed the statement without reading it. He had no intention of denying what he had done to her. The police had accepted that the fire itself had been an accident. The police still needed Becky to press charges though. Even with the admission of guilt, it would not be worth taking the case to court without a victim who was willing to testify. Sergeant Cleaver had found Becky uncooperative when he had interviewed her the day before, but he was hoping that she had thought about it overnight and would agree to proceed with the case.

Even without the assault they had enough on Tony to put him away for a few years. They had searched his premises and had found drugs and stolen goods in a garage he rented. They also found evidence that he had been killing the local cats.

'We've got enough on you to send you down for at least eight years,' said Cleaver. 'You might as well make it easier for the both of us and just confess to everything.'

Tony was wracked with guilt over what had happened. It was not what he had planned. He had hurt the one woman he had ever loved. He had nothing left now. Esther had left him, Becky would never forgive him, he had no money and even his best friend was to marry the mother of his child. Then he remembered Sandra Palmer and the hundred grand that Becky had given her. He leaned across the table and looked the sergeant straight in the eye. He grinned.

'You've got nothing on me,' he said.

*

Becky walked through Homerton. The town baked in the sunshine and a solitary cloud floated in the blue sky. On the board in front of the newsagent the headline from the local paper said: *Sunny Days Are Here Again.*

Becky phoned the police and told them she did not want to press charges against Tony. She wanted to begin her life again, or more to start it for the first time because it felt as if the last five years had been lived under a cloud. There had been this terrible shadow over everything she did. Now she had the chance to be free and to put the past behind her once and for all. She did not want a court case forcing her to relive what had happened. Besides, she did not want to be the one to send Tony to prison. She had ruined enough lives already and could not bear to blame herself for destroying another. There would also be questions, cross-examination of her relationship with Tony, her feelings for him, whether she had willingly gone with him to the hut to have sex. Even with a guilty plea there would be questions. Becky was not even sure in her own mind what had happened that night. She just wanted to forget the whole thing and move on.

Becky helped Esther pack her things and they waited together in the sunshine for the taxi that was going to take her to Acle and the train to Cambridge.

As Esther was getting into the cab, she turned and said, 'Well, this is it.'

'Not an end but a beginning,' said Becky.

Esther hesitated, as if she needed to say something that she had been wanting to say for years. 'The truth is, we all loved you too much, Becks. Each one of us: Tony, James, Stuart. Me. That's why we did what we did all those years ago and why this town has been shrouded in darkness since you left. I guess we just have to accept that some love affairs were never meant to be.'

Esther quickly kissed Becky on the cheek then climbed into the cab and left Homerton forever.

Becky had thought about confessing to the police about the death of Mr Palmer. It was something she had considered over the years, but she had never been brave enough to do it. Now with the police questioning her over the assault, she had the perfect opportunity. She had even started telling them how she and Tony had been boyfriend and girlfriend when she was in the sixth form at college and how is wife Esther had been her best friend. She even mentioned how they used to go to the fisherman's hut when they were younger. She told them she had left Homerton five years ago. But none of it registered with the police officers and they failed to make any connection with what happened then. They were too young to remember or had not been in the area at the time. They were not interested in the past; all they wanted was to clear up current cases so they could achieve their targets.

Becky had decided not to push it further. She thought about James and how he was struggling to keep the garage afloat as well as caring for Nick. She thought about Stuart and Sam and the new baby and how it deserved to be brought up with a dad regardless of whether Stuart or Tony was the actual father. What good would it do to reopen the death of Mr Palmer now, after all these years? In one way or another, they had all paid the price for what happened.

Becky went to visit James to thank him for saving her life and to say goodbye. He was playing a shooting game on the TV with Nick.

'How is it?' he asked, inspecting the scar on her face.

'Still sore. But at least the burning pain has stopped. If it wasn't for you, I could have been burnt alive – Tony as well.'

'I'm sure *he* would have escaped somehow.'

'I can never thank you enough, James. You really are my hero.'

'What on earth were you doing with him up there, Becks? You know what a bastard he is. Always has been.'

'We all make mistakes,' said Becky. 'Things got out of hand. I just wanted to say goodbye to him. He was pretty shaken up, you know. With what happened to Esther. I've just said goodbye to her. I'm glad she is starting again. You know she is moving to Cambridge?'

'There is going to be no one left in this town soon.'

'You've still got Stuart,' Becky said.

James shook his head. 'He's got Sam and the baby now.' Nick tugged at James's arm to ask him to explain some instructions on the screen and James patiently went through them with him.

'And how are you, Nick?' asked Becky. Nick held out his arms to show her where they had been burnt and she turned her face and pointed to the scar on her cheek. They both pulled a sad face and shrugged and then Nick returned to his game.

'I'd better go. I'm getting the train back to London tonight.' She hugged James and asked him to say goodbye to Stuart for her. Nick came over and joined in the hug, throwing his arms around the two of them.

They were taking down the For Sale sign. The driver lifted Becky's bags into the boot of the cab. It was raining more heavily now, and she dashed back up the path to drop the cottage keys in through the letterbox. She ran back down the path, and the driver opened the back door for her.

He turned around from the front seat. 'Great Yarmouth Station?' the driver asked. 'You don't remember me, do you? Viktor. I drove you here. It must have been a couple of weeks ago now, maybe a bit more. It was really tipping down and I nearly got lost on all those country roads.' He leaned into the dashboard and wiped the screen. 'Not much better tonight. No wonder people take their bleeding holidays in Spain. Who can blame them, eh?'

The taxi crunched over the gravel drive and turned into the town. Becky could see Viktor looking at her in the rear-view mirror. Making up a story in his head about what she had done for the past couple of weeks, how she had injured her face. He was itching to talk to her but something about the way she looked told him now was not the time. He turned on the radio. The wipers swished across the windscreen. As they left Homerton, Becky turned away from the rain-streaked window. She could not bear to look back.

19

After the Fire

'It's Becky!' said Nick, pointing at the television. A broad grin sliced his round face. He slapped his thigh. 'I told you she didn't leave us. She's here, look.'

And she was. James swivelled round and saw her face fill the screen. She looked as beautiful as ever. The camera lingered on the close-up. Becky was laughing and sweeping back her hair in that way she did. She was on one of those semi-acted, semi-reality TV shows called *Down in Dalston*.

It was six years since James had last seen Becky, six years since she had left Homerton following the fire at the cabin on the cliffs. 'You're right, Nick. She didn't leave us, did she.'

A month later, an invitation arrived unexpectedly. It was from Becky. Inside the envelope was one of those white printed invite cards with a gold border. It said: *You are cordially invited to celebrate Becky Sullivan's big three zero.* There was a date and an address in part of London James had never heard of. On the back of the card, Becky had written in her girly, looping hand: *Please come, James. I miss the old gang,* and she had signed it with four big kisses.

The party was in a shabby Victorian house in north London that Becky shared with another woman from the show. The walls were painted acid-yellow and the floorboards were grass green. People's coats had been tossed into the bathtub. Bottles of booze were piled up on the kitchen table. The house was packed. Everyone was trying to look beautiful and sophisticated and most of them succeeded. James felt awkward and out of place. They all seemed to know each other or pretended to. James put down the bottle of gin he had brought.

'You came, James,' said Becky brightly. She kissed him on the cheek. 'I really hoped you would, but my hopes weren't that high. I thought you'd never leave Homerton, not even for a night.' She stood back slightly and smiled at him again. 'What a big adventure. A wild party in the big city. Now, you come with me,' she said, finding his hand. 'I don't want you skulking around and not talking to anybody. I'm sure there a plenty of pretty actresses who would love to meet a country boy. Let's enjoy ourselves.'

'So, how are things?' asked Becky. They had come back into the kitchen from the whirl of the party.

'Things are good,' said James. 'Homerton is very trendy now. We've got a couple of posh restaurants, and the old cottages are selling like hot cakes. I'm surprised you haven't read about it in your magazines. They're calling us the next Wells-next-the-Sea.' He smiled and Becky did not know whether he was joking or not.

'The garage packed with sports cars, focaccia in the minimart...' teased Becky.

'That's right. You wouldn't recognise the place. We couldn't afford to grow up there now.'

Becky felt a stabbing desire to return to Homerton, but it soon passed. She was not young anymore and did not know where her youth had gone. 'And who *is* left there now?'

'Me, of course, and Nick. I wheel him out occasionally just to scare the weekenders. I tell them lots of kids in the town were born like Nick; that they reckon it is something in the air, some sort of pollution from the refinery over at Becton. You should see their faces!'

'You are still looking after Nick then?'

'I can't not do, can I?' James shrugged. 'He won't be around for much longer, not with his condition, and I couldn't bear to put him in a care home.'

Becky thought James was being pretty heroic about his situation, but he was keen to move the focus on to someone else. 'I haven't heard from Esther for a couple of years now,' he said. 'Last time I heard she was working in a prison. I keep in touch with Stuart and Samantha though.' He took his wallet from his jacket and flipped it open. He pulled out a small photograph. 'I brought this along to show you.' It was a picture of Stuart and Sam with their son. It was uncanny. The boy looked like a young Tony. The resemblance was striking.

'They've had another one since,' said James. 'A little girl. Now they are quite the family.'

'You know I wasn't talking about them, James. It's Tony I want to know about.'

'How can you even think about him after what he did?'

'Is he back in Homerton?'

'He is. He came out of prison about a year ago. Three and a half years for drug dealing and killing cats. Can you believe that? I didn't realise he was such a sick bastard. Those poor cats, what on earth possessed him to do that?'

'It was something to do with his mother,' said Becky. 'He hated all those cats she had around.'

'Sounds like you're making excuses for him, Becky. Anyhow, he's back with his mother now, no doubt making her life hell.'

'I was attracted to him,' said Becky. 'Maybe I even loved him. Of course, it's different now, after what he did, but I was attracted to him. I know you find that hard to believe, but there was an energy about him, a furious energy, which made me feel alive when I was with him. He was hypnotic and I was spellbound. I knew he was a bastard from the start, that there was something bad deep inside of him, but I saw it as, like, you know, a sort of sickness. I thought he was ill, that he had an incurable illness.'

'And you wanted to cure him,' sneered James. *She still thinks it is a game*, he thought.

'No, not that. The truth is, I was as bad as him. I wanted the same things. He didn't force me to do anything. I thought he was my escape from Homerton. I imagined we were Bonnie and Clyde going off to have adventures together.' She gave an embarrassed giggle. 'And then when I came back to sell the cottage, oh, I don't know what it was. I guess I was feeling pretty mixed up at the time. I was lonely and seeing him again, well it sort of ignited something. I felt sorry for him in a way. He looked so trapped, like he was in a cage. I don't know, I realise none of this makes any sense, that you probably think I am a stupid cow or worse. But we don't always do the sensible thing do we? Life's not like that. It's not all about doing the right thing. It is the wrong things that make us who we are.'

'I don't think that's true,' said James. 'The wrong things can destroy us. It's not all about you, Becky.'

Becky knew what he was talking about. 'It was a long time ago, James. Surely we've earned the right to forget about it now. It's hung over us for long enough.'

'I don't know what you want me to say. It feels like you want somebody to tell you it's not your fault. That we are not to blame. We killed a man, for Christ's sake, then we pretended nothing happened. It's ruined my life, Becky, and I think it might have ruined yours as well.'

'That's so unfair, James. We were just kids growing up in a place where you can't breathe, a place that smothers you half to death. We didn't know what we were doing.'

'Homerton's no different from anywhere else, Becky. It's us that are different.'

'Maybe we are all looking for excuses,' said Becky. The party carried on around them, but James did not feel in the mood anymore. He knew now that he would never be anything more than a friend to Becky. 'I don't want to lose touch with you,' she said. It felt like a goodbye. James decided to leave. He promised to keep in touch. He kissed Becky on the cheek, breathed in the smell of her skin.

James picked his way down the stairs and along the hallway. He went out into the cold, fresh air, leaving the thud of the party behind him. The city was alive; lights blazed in the darkness, he could hear sirens and trains and the honking of car horns. There was laughter and shouting. The air smelt of smoke and takeaways and rubbish. James felt elated, but lonely too. He decided to walk to Liverpool Street Station and to catch the first train to Norwich in the morning.

*

Esther sometimes thought about the others, but not for long. After graduating, she had worked as a psychologist for the prison service but two years ago she had given it up when she realised all the men started to look like Tony Fletcher and she no longer cared what motivated them. She bought a little bistro in Cambridge that had red-and-white tablecloths and brass lamps and smelt of garlic and herbs. On sunny days she imagined she was in the South of France.

Esther had been married for a couple of years to a kind and gentle man who she had met at a French evening class, but she left because she was bored and had decided she was no longer prepared to accept second best in her life. She still felt guilty about it. He had deserved better, she knew that, but she had to put herself first. Now she drank alone, and she still wore her wedding ring to deter potential suitors.

It was a quiet Tuesday afternoon when the door of the bistro tinkled open, and a family bustled inside. There was a man and a woman, a young boy and a toddler in a pushchair. The man was carrying a small suitcase as well as pushing the buggy. Esther saw that it was Stuart straight away and she recognised the woman was Samantha.

The young student waitress found them a table and Stuart settled the kids into the chairs. He leaned over and kissed Sam on the cheek. 'Looks OK, doesn't it?'

Sam glanced round the room. There were little vases on the tables with sprigs of herbs in them. Tom Waits played quietly in the background. A cat was curled up in a basket by the serving counter. Sam scanned the menu, worrying what the kids would eat. 'It looks expensive,' she said, 'perhaps we should find somewhere else.'

'No, no. This is fine,' said Stuart. He looked a bit uncomfortable but very happy. He had taken them to Cambridge for a few days as a birthday treat for Samantha. He was now a supervisor at the bus company and for the first time in years they had a little money to spare.

Stuart's face had fattened out like an overripe fruit. His hair had gone thin on top. A wedding ring pinched his chubby finger. For a moment, Esther hesitated. Seeing Stuart had been a shock, and she was not sure whether she could face talking to him after all these years. She took a deep breath and told the waitress she would handle this one. She went over to the table.

'Hi, Stuart.'

Samantha kicked him under the table and Stuart looked up. His eyes popped with surprise and his face blushed and twitched, like a child caught doing something naughty.

'You work here?' he blurted out. His face coloured even more, this time with embarrassment. 'I didn't mean… It's just I thought you worked in a prison.'

Esther smiled. 'I don't work here,' she said. 'I own the place. I brought it a couple of years ago. Didn't you see the name outside?'

Stuart looked at the windows. *Esther's* was etched on to the glass and he saw now the name on the top of the menus.

'I see you two are still happily married.' Esther gave a Sam a friendly nod. Motherhood clearly suited her. Sam looked creamy and soft. Esther smiled at the toddler then turned to the boy. He was engrossed in a small action figure he was playing with but, sensing her eyes on him, he looked up and Esther was startled by his resemblance to Tony Fletcher. She quickly turned away as if he had some hideous deformity.

'This is Caitlin,' said Stuart, indicating the girl. 'And you know Tyson.' He had noticed the shock on Esther's face. It shocked him too how much Tyson looked like his father, but he had come to terms with it. He asked Esther if she was doing OK. But Esther knew that what he really meant was whether she had come to terms with what happened. Whether she was coping with the past.

'I've moved on,' said Esther. 'Things are good. But what about you? Are still living in Homerton?'

Stuart said he was, and that James was still running the garage and they met up for a drink every few weeks.

'And what about Tony?'

'He's back but I avoid him if I can, most of the town does.

He would be better off getting out of Homerton – nobody wants him there – but it's as if he sticks around to deliberately annoy people. And what about you and Becky?' said Stuart, not wanting to talk about Tony anymore.

'I haven't seen her for several years. Somebody told me she is on the TV.' Esther regretted losing touch with Becky. Every now and then she thought of tracking her down and making contact, but Esther was happy for the first time in her life and she did not want reminders of the past to ruin that. Esther had learnt that regrets are stupid, and that the important thing was to live for the moment. She was glad when Stuart and Sam finished their meal. She gave it to them on the house and told them that they must come back someday but she hoped they didn't. She watched them as they walked down the road towards the station. Their lives seemed to be turning out alright in the end. Stuart was happily married with a family, James had kept the business going, Becky had found fame at last, and she had her lovely little bistro. She was more than content, she was happy. It was a glorious afternoon and as the sun lit up the inside of the bistro; Esther's face broke into a joyous grin.

20

Detective Sergeant Cleaver cursed as he slipped on the muddy path that led to the top of the cliffs. The rain was swirling down from the night sky and sharp gusts of wind battered the coast. He felt a fool as he stumbled up the hill and cursed the council for not putting in a proper path.

The police spotlights sparkled in the rain as he reached the top, illuminating the shell of the fisherman's cabin. The area was sealed off with tape that fluttered violently in the wind. Silhouetted figures moved around in the darkness. The detective took a deep breath. *I am getting too old for this game*, he thought. He should have been at home with his feet up in front of the telly.

One of the keen young policemen came bounding over to him, rain glistening on his grinning face. 'They found him a couple of hours ago, just after six; some poor sod out walking his dog, it was. The pathologist's taking a look now but it's clear he drank himself to death.'

'Oh, it is, is it?'

'Seriously, sir. It's like a bloody bottle bank in there.'

'And we are sure it's Tony Fletcher?' asked the detective sergeant as they trudged towards the hut.

'Positive. He looks a mess though.'

Sergeant Cleaver felt the rain drip from his nose. 'Nobody would look good after a couple of hours out in this bloody weather.'

A tarpaulin was pulled across the top of the hut and the rain hammered down on it, making a terrible racket. It was freezing. Tony's body was slumped against the end wall of the main room of the hut. Empty bottles were scattered around the body. He was dressed in a few wretched clothes. The photographer had just finished and was packing away. Cleaver nodded to him as if to say, "It's on nights like this…".

Tony Fletcher's face was fixed in the glare of a spotlight.

'There's nothing to suggest he was murdered,' said the policeman beside him, with a hint of disappointment in his voice. 'No weapon, no injuries, no sign of a struggle…'

'At least not with anyone else,' said Cleaver.

'…It's suicide really, isn't it? Slow suicide. Who knows why they do it. They're like those dogs, you know, who skulk off to die alone.'

The policeman was enjoying the whole thing too much for Cleaver's liking and he went over to talk to the pathologist.

'My guess is it was a number of things: heart attack, drugs overdose, alcohol poisoning, hypothermia. Take your pick as to which one came first. I don't suppose it matters that much. He died about four hours ago probably, but it's difficult to tell in this weather. I'll let you have a full report tomorrow.'

The detective sergeant stared down at the crumpled body lying in the mud and surrounded by broken glass. It was not a good way for any man to go. There was nothing more that could be done tonight. He indicated to one of the policemen that the body could be taken away to the morgue. He looked up at the sky, trying to decide if there was any chance the rain would stop. He wanted to get away as quickly as possible, to get home and scrub himself clean in a hot bath.

Phil Parkin came into the Fisherman's Return and announced, 'They've found Tony up at the hut. He's dead.' For a moment, the pub fell silent, although some of the regulars had smiles on their faces and they were soon offering to buy each other drinks.

I decided to hang around for a few days until the funeral. It was a week of damp, grey weather but somehow the town seemed more cheerful, as if it had come out of a bad cold and could smell the fresh air again. You noticed it in the way people greeted you in the mini-market and the tearoom. They were all talking about how the council had finally agreed to demolish the fisherman's cabin on the cliffs.

The local newspaper ran a brief story about the body of a local man being found dead in an abandoned fisherman's cabin. They said the cause of death was alcohol poisoning and that the man was forty and single. It seemed a mean obituary for a man who had been such a well-known figure in the town but nobody else seemed bothered. They were glad he was gone.

The funeral took place a couple of days later. It was a cold, drizzly, windswept Friday and the crematorium in Acle looked grey and depressing. I could not help but see the irony in Tony Fletcher finally being turned to ashes. There were only four of us in attendance, me, Tony's elderly mother, James Larner and a frail-looking but elegant woman in her forties. She was too thin and the black dress she was wearing was too big so she seems shrivelled inside it, but she had clearly once been very beautiful. Even now, she could have graced the pages of a high-end magazine. Her face was pale, but she wore bright scarlet lipstick. I assumed this was the infamous Becky Sullivan. It was not clear whether she and James had come to pay their last respects or to confirm that Tony was finally dead and gone. The service was quick and dismal. I was sitting along from Tony's mother, and she showed no emotion at all. James and Becky were on the other side of the aisle, and I could not see them clearly but as the cheap coffin rolled into the blazing furnace I heard Becky Sullivan gasp and saw James lay his hand gently on hers, as if to comfort her. We sat there is silence. Outside there was only the sound of rain.

About the author

David Ford was born in Devon and lives in East London. For thirty-five years he worked in central government, mainly as a senior policy advisor on crime issues in the Home Office. A collection of his poetry has been published by the Happenstance Press and his first novel, *Come Sunday*, was published in 2023. David is married with two daughters.